Join Us at the ~~Covered Bridge~~
on New Year's Eve
as We Commemorate
One Hundred Years of History
and Usher in a New Era
for Jasper Gulch!

We never thought we'd see the day!
The Shaws and the Masseys have been reunited, the time capsule has been found, and, as we celebrate the actual day of Jasper Gulch's founding, we will be reopening the Beaver Creek Bridge. We here in Jasper Gulch couldn't be happier, and we suspect that somewhere, Lucy Shaw is smiling down on us. She'll be smiling even harder when she sees that Robin Frazier is keeping company with pastor Ethan Johnson. But do you want to know *why*? Keep turning pages and find out as Big Sky Centennial reaches its heartwarming conclusion!

* * *

Big Sky Centennial:
A small town rich in history…and love.

Her Montana Cowboy by Valerie Hansen—*July 2014*
His Montana Sweetheart by Ruth Logan Herne—*August 2014*
Her Montana Twins by Carolyne Aarsen—*September 2014*
His Montana Bride by Brenda Minton—*October 2014*
His Montana Homecoming by Jenna Mindel—*November 2014*
Her Montana Christmas by Arlene James—*December 2014*

Books by Arlene James

Love Inspired

*The Perfect Wedding
*An Old-Fashioned Love
*A Wife Worth Waiting For
*With Baby in Mind
 The Heart's Voice
 To Heal a Heart
 Deck the Halls
 A Family to Share
 Butterfly Summer
 A Love So Strong
 When Love Comes Home
 A Mommy in Mind
**His Small-Town Girl
**Her Small-Town Hero
**Their Small-Town Love
 †Anna Meets Her Match

†A Match Made in Texas
 A Mother's Gift
  "Dreaming of a Family"
†Baby Makes a Match
†An Unlikely Match
 The Sheriff's Runaway Bride
†Second Chance Match
†Building a Perfect Match
 Carbon Copy Cowboy
 Love in Bloom
†His Ideal Match
†The Bachelor Meets His Match
 Her Montana Christmas

*Everyday Miracles
**Eden, OK
†Chatam House

ARLENE JAMES

says, "Camp meetings, mission work and church attendance permeate my Oklahoma childhood memories. It was a golden time, which sustains me yet. However, only as a young widowed mother did I truly begin growing in my personal relationship with the Lord. Through adversity He has blessed me in countless ways, one of which is a second marriage so loving and romantic it still feels like courtship!"

After thirty-three years in Texas, Arlene James now resides in Bella Vista, Arkansas, with her beloved husband. Even after seventy-five novels, her need to write is greater than ever, a fact that frankly amazes her, as she's been at it since the eighth grade. She loves to hear from readers, and can be reached via her website, www.arlenejames.com.

Her Montana Christmas

Arlene James

HARLEQUIN® LOVE INSPIRED®

Special thanks and acknowledgment to Arlene James
for her contribution to the Big Sky Centennial miniseries.

Recycling programs
for this product may
not exist in your area.

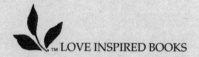

ISBN-13: 978-0-373-87925-0

Her Montana Christmas

www.Harlequin.com

Printed in U.S.A.

Many, Lord my God, are the wonders You have done, the things You planned for us. None can compare with You; were I to speak and tell of Your deeds, they would be too many to declare.

—Psalms 40:5

Chapter One

The first day of December in Jasper Gulch, Montana, sparkled like diamonds. Pastor Ethan Johnson stood in front of the small, weathered parsonage that had been his home these past five months and inhaled early-morning air sharp enough to cut his California-born lungs to shreds, but not even the cold could dim his joy in the day. The snow from November's freakish storm had finally melted, power had been fully restored and the distinct aura of Christmas permeated the atmosphere.

Ethan was excited to celebrate his first real Christmas as the pastor of Mountainview Church of the Savior. He loved the Lord. He loved being a pastor. He loved the people here in Jasper Gulch. He loved the beauty of Montana. He even loved the church building itself.

The unorthodox log-plank structure had taken on the shape of a cross over the years. It wasn't at all what one expected or usually pictured when thinking of a church, and yet it fit its purpose supremely well. The belfry contained two brass bells, sadly no longer in use, and four large speakers through which the recordings of bells were played daily. Ethan admired everything about the place, from its broad plank walkways, to its steep, wood-shingled roofs, perhaps because it was his first pastorate or perhaps because it truly was a special place.

The town, though small with just nine hundred or so residents, was certainly unique. Jasper Gulch had been engaged in a six-month-long celebration of its centennial, starting on the Fourth of July and ending on the last day of this year. It seemed to Ethan that the Christmas services should reflect that motif. The idea had come to him the previous night as he'd prayed over his preparations for the holidays, and he knew just where to get the information necessary to make his first Christmas in Jasper Gulch a success in keeping with the centennial theme.

Casting a last fond look at the church building, Ethan swung down into the seat of his dependable nine-year-old dark green Subaru Forester. He could walk over to the museum, but he didn't know what he might be bringing back with him, books, papers or other media, so he drove. Already many Christmas decorations were out, thanks to Faith Shaw, the mayor's eldest daughter.

Dale Massey, a fabulously wealthy scion of one of the town's two founding families, had come out from New York City to participate in last month's centennial Homecoming celebration, only to find himself stranded in Jasper Gulch by the unexpected storm. Faith, a daughter of the other founding family, the Shaws, had convinced the community's residents to pitch together to give Dale a taste of a small-town Montana Christmas. As a result, Faith and Dale were now engaged to be married on Christmas night—and Ethan had started thinking in earnest about the true Christmas celebration to come.

Mayor Jackson Shaw seemed pleased to have his eldest daughter marry. For a time, he'd appeared determined to foster a romance between her and Ethan. Apparently, everyone in town wanted to make a match for the new pastor. Much to Ethan's dismay, they'd thrown every eligible female within traveling distance at him. Thankfully, Shaw seemed less eager to marry off Ethan than he did his own children, for the man had gotten his way with three of the five. Ethan had found that the mayor usually did get his way, but his future son-in-law was bucking him on reopening the Beaver Creek Bridge.

From what Ethan could gather, the bridge had been closed since a Shaw relative had driven off it to her death in an automobile accident nearly ninety years earlier. Apparently, Jackson's grandfather had promised *his* father that the bridge would never be reopened, and Jackson had renewed that pledge when he'd first assumed his place as mayor, an office that the Shaws had held for generations.

Other, more forward-thinking citizens pointed out that, with the bridge closed, Jasper Gulch could be accessed by only one road, but Jackson Shaw had repeatedly beaten back attempts to repair and reopen the bridge—until Dale Massey had magnanimously offered to underwrite the project on his own.

Personally, Ethan thought it a shame to let an eighty-eight-year-old tragedy dictate public policy, but he couldn't help feeling some sympathy for Mayor Shaw. The man was trying to pull off six months of centennial celebration that had been missing its centerpiece from the beginning. On the very first weekend, the time capsule that the whole town had gathered to open had gone missing. Since then, the town had suffered several instances of vandalism and more than one cryptic note hinting that the capsule had contained a treasure and was connected with the initials L.S.

A local teenager by the name of Lilibeth Shoemaker had fallen under suspicion, but she insisted that she'd had nothing to do with the notes or the disappearance of the time capsule. Though she'd been officially exonerated, a few still harbored suspicions of her based on her initials alone, but Ethan certainly wasn't about to judge her guilty on such flimsy evidence. Most believed that a local man named Pete Daniels was to blame because he'd suddenly left town without explanation.

The time capsule had finally turned up, opened. It contained some historical documents, photos and mementos, but nothing of any market value. Ethan doubted they'd ever know the truth about the time capsule's contents or who had taken it, and he, for one, did not really care. He would be glad to see the centennial celebrations come to an end on New Year's Eve with the burial of a new time capsule, the official opening of the museum and the reopening of the Beaver Creek Bridge—unless the mayor found some way to prevent the latter. Again.

After parking in front of the museum, Ethan took a moment to enjoy the new building. A few folks had complained that the structure was nothing more than a brown sheet-iron pole barn with an Old West–style front attached, complete with hitching rails, but Ethan figured that a town the size of Jasper Gulch was blessed to have a bona fide museum of any sort. He got out of the car and, finding the front door unlocked, went inside.

A wide reception area, with an unattended Y-shaped desk, branched off into two hallways. Hearing the unmistakable sound of a copy machine at work in the distance, Ethan dumped his down coat, wool muffler and gloves on the desk and walked along the left hallway toward the sound.

The slender feminine figure at the copy machine jolted him. She wasn't Olivia Franklin McGuire, the curator, though the purple sweater and black slacks seemed vaguely familiar. The long, straight tail of wheat-colored hair, caught at her nape with a black barrette, swung between the curves of her shoulder blades as she caught the papers shooting from the end of the machine.

He put on his best pastor's smile and said, "Excuse me."

She whirled around, pale hair flying. Her peaked brows, several shades darker than her hair, arched high over rich blue eyes as round as marbles. He spotted a tiny flat dark mole just under the tip of her left brow, which she reached up to touch with one finger, calling attention to her perfect nose and lips the color of a dusky rose, the bottom fuller than the upper, with a little seam in the middle as if God had created it in two perfect halves and knit it together.

"Ah, yes. Robin Frazier."

They'd met more than once. She'd been attending church semiregularly for months now, and they'd spoken on several occasions, but never more than a few passing words. She seemed a serious, studious sort, despite the youthfulness of her face. He'd first seen her at a distance and taken her for a teenager, then wondered why he didn't see her with the other kids. Someone had finally told him that she was a graduate student visiting Jasper Gulch on some sort of project.

"Pastor Johnson," she said, several seconds having ticked by. "Can I help you?"

He waved a hand at the papers she held. "Material for your..." He couldn't remember exactly what her project was. "I'm sorry. Something to do with genealogy, isn't it?"

She stared at the papers in her hand as if resigning herself to speaking to him. Then her deep blue eyes met his, and a funny thing happened inside his chest. At the same time, she spoke.

"This has to do with the centennial. I've been hired to help out here at the museum."

Since he'd moved to Jasper Gulch, all the eligible females in town had cast lures of one sort or another in Ethan's direction, but this one seemed reticent, almost wary of him. He should have felt relieved about that. Instead, he felt…disappointed, even a bit irritated, though God knew he wasn't in the market for a wife.

"Really?" He put on a smile. "That's great. I hope it means you'll be joining the church."

She just looked at him without answer for several heartbeats before asking again, "Can I help you with something?"

"It's about Christmas," he said, not at all put off. He was used to people stonewalling, hedging, even outright prevarication when it came to the subject of church attendance. He took his openings when, where and how he found them and left the results to the Lord. "I'm hoping to have a historical kind of Christmas this year. You know, sort of do my part for the centennial. The thing is, being from California and fairly new to the area, I have no real idea what Christmas might have been like around here a hundred years ago."

"Well," she said, "let's see what information we can find for you then."

Ethan grinned. It looked as if he had come to the right place. And maybe, when all was said and done, he'd find himself with a new congregant, as well.

Robin didn't know why the young pastor set her on edge, but he had from the first moment that she'd met him almost five months ago now. He wasn't just handsome; he was a nice man, almost *too* nice. Something about him made a person want to confide in him, even when he wasn't wearing his clerical collar, like now, or maybe it was just that she wanted to confide in *someone*.

She hated being in Jasper Gulch under false pretenses, and the longer it went on, the worse she felt, but she dared not truthfully identify herself at this late date. Too much had happened. She couldn't step forward now and tell the truth without raising everyone's suspicions about her motives. After everything that had gone on—the theft of the time capsule, the vandalism and mysterious notes, the investigation and the disappearance of Pete Daniels, the sudden reappearance of the time capsule and all the mysteries that she and Olivia had uncovered about the past, not to mention the secrets that Robin alone knew—everyone would think that she was after something. It didn't help that a member of the extremely wealthy Massey family had shown up on the scene, either. Connections to wealth, as Robin knew all too well, inspired a certain type of grasping, clinging hanger-on.

Sometimes Robin thought it would be best if she just left town as quietly as she'd arrived in July, but she couldn't quite make herself go. Not yet. And go back to what? Her parents and grandparents had never disguised their disappointment in her. With her great-grandmother Lillian dead, she couldn't find much reason to go back to New Mexico, and Great-Grandma Lillian had known it would be that way, too. Why else on her deathbed would she have urged Robin to come here and find what other family she might have left?

"So the church was here even before the town was officially founded," the pastor said, laying aside the newspaper article she'd printed off for him. "Interesting. I wonder if any of the original building still stands."

Pulled from her reverie, Robin shrugged. "Apparently there were several homes and a small log church in the area when Ezra Shaw and Silas Massey decided to formally incorporate the town and draw up a charter. I'm sure I can find something about the church building, given enough time."

"I'd appreciate that, even though it's mostly curiosity on my part," Pastor Johnson told her, smiling warmly. "I'm most interested in the vestibule and the belfry."

"The rock part at the front of the church?"

"Exactly. Did you know there are actual bells up there in the belfry?"

"You mean they're not just for show?"

He shook his head. "I have to wonder why we never use perfectly good bells. I mean, recorded bells are fine for every day, but what a treat it would be to pull the ropes on real bells once in a while. I wonder why the church stopped using them."

"That is a puzzle. I can look into it, if you like."

"I'd love to know, but I hate to put you to any extra trouble."

She shrugged. "I don't mind. I like solving puzzles."

He would understand that about her if he knew what mysteries had brought her here to Jasper Gulch, but then perhaps it was best that no one here knew.

Her plan had seemed so simple in the beginning. Come to town under the guise of a graduate student doing research for a thesis on genealogy. Find proof to support her claims. Show the proof. Be greeted warmly by family who previously hadn't known she existed.

Five months into the project, she now realized that her proof wasn't likely to be any more welcome than she would be, that her motives could easily be questioned and that she could well come off looking like a schemer and a liar. She bitterly regretted the route she'd taken to this point. She had feared being jeered at in the beginning, but at least she could have conducted her research in the open, then once the proof had been found, all would have been well. Now...now people trusted her, people to whom she must reveal herself as a liar. What a fool she had been.

"I appreciate any information you can give me," Pastor Johnson told Robin forthrightly, again breaking into her troubled thoughts.

He had the kindest brown eyes and the most open, engaging smile she'd ever seen. Everything about him exuded warmth, even on this first day of December. His California origin showed in the burnished brown of his short, neat hair and bronzed skin. In fact, Robin could easily picture him walking barefoot in the surf with his sleeves and pant legs rolled up, the tail of his chambray shirt pulled free of the waistband of his jeans. He looked younger without his ministerial collar, almost boyish, despite the faint crinkles that fanned out from the corners of his deep-set eyes. Something about the way his long, straight nose flattened at the end intrigued her, as did the manner in which his squared chin added a certain strength to his face.

"What?" he asked, his lips widening to show a great many strong, white teeth.

She shook her head, embarrassed to have been caught staring. "I, um, I'll see what I can find and get back to you."

"Excellent. Can I give you my personal cell number, as well as the numbers at the church and the parsonage? That way you're bound to reach me."

"Oh, of course. That would be fine." She pulled out her phone and tapped in the numbers as he gave them to her. When she looked up again, he had his own phone in his hand.

"Mind if I take your numbers, too? In case I have any questions?"

Robin was aware of her heart speeding up, which was ridiculous. He was a minister, a man of God. He wasn't hitting on her. In fact, he probably intended to call and invite her to join the church again. She wouldn't mind if he did. She just didn't know if she could do that; she might not be staying in Jasper Gulch for much longer.

"Uh, sure." She gave him her cell number, though mobile coverage was not the best here, as well as the numbers at the museum and her residence, such as it was. He

saved them to his contacts list before pocketing the tiny
phone again.

"There now," he said. "I have a lead on the information I need to make this a grand centennial Christmas,
I've found a kindred spirit to help me solve a puzzle and
I've got the phone number of one of the prettiest ladies in
town. That's what I call an excellent morning's work." He
turned a full circle, walking backward a step or two, as he
headed for the door. "I look forward to hearing from you."

He was out of sight and halfway down the hall before
Robin's own laughter caught up with her, and her heartbeat
still hadn't slowed one iota. It had, in fact, sped up! Perhaps that was why she called him later when she stumbled
across information concerning the church bells.

A tidbit in the local newspaper from early 1925 had
reported that the bells had been deemed unsafe due to
problems with the crosspiece in the belfry and would
"henceforth be silenced to prevent any startling and ca-
lamitous accidents." The reporter had gone on to quote
a deacon as insisting that rumors suggesting this decision had to do with the "decampment of Silas Massey and
his wife" were "scurrilous and mean-spirited," which led
Robin to wonder aloud if the aforementioned rumors had
anything to do with the bank failure.

"Bank failure?" Ethan echoed.

Robin mentally cringed. "Sorry. I wouldn't want you
to think I was gossiping. Speculation is part and parcel of
historical research, I'm afraid. It's just that we've uncovered evidence of some trouble at the bank founded by the
Shaws and the Masseys here in Jasper Gulch. The timeline
says everything's connected. First, the Masseys pulled out.
Then the rumors started flying about the bank being in-
solvent. Right after that, the bells were determined to be
unsafe, with a deacon at the church insisting that the decision had nothing to do with the Masseys leaving town.

It seems as if Ezra Shaw was quoted in every edition of the newspaper around that time saying that the bank was solvent and all was fine, but when the crash came in '32, it failed spectacularly and was reported to be woefully undercapitalized. Shaw was quoted as saying that for him it was just a long nightmare come to an end but that he felt badly for his neighbors and depositors, whom he promised to help as much as he was able. It just seems logical that Massey had something to do with the whole situation."

"So you're saying that Silas Massey either forced Ezra Shaw to buy him out, which caused the bank to be undercapitalized, or he stole—"

"I'm just telling you what we've uncovered," Robin interrupted smoothly.

"However it came about," Ethan said, "there were bound to be some hard feelings. I think it's worth looking into to see if the bells might have been a gift to the church from the Masseys." He added that he was going to dig into some old file cabinets tucked into a closet in a back room. "I might find something of interest to the museum."

Robin remembered that, and the next day when she found a website that showed details, as well as written instructions, for re-creating exactly the sort of decorations the pastor would need to provide a centennial-style Christmas for his congregation, she decided to print off photos and drive over to the church with them on her lunch hour. She and Olivia had their hands full getting the displays at the museum ready for viewing, but Olivia's husband, Jack, had come into town from his ranch on an errand, so the two of them were having an early lunch together, and that gave Robin a bit of free time.

She parked right in front of the church, grabbed the file folder in which she'd stashed the printouts and hopped out of her metallic-blue hybrid coupe. Stepping up on the plank walkway, she hurried to the white-painted front door of the church. It swung open easily. She walked into the cool, strangely silent vestibule and let her eyes adjust from the bright sunlight.

The vestibule usually rang with noise and always seemed dark, despite the twin brass chandeliers hanging from the ceiling. Not today, however. Today, a shaft of light illuminated the very center of the wide space, along with the slender metal ladder that descended from the belfry. She looked up to find an open trapdoor in the vestibule ceiling.

"Pastor?" she called, amazed at the way her voice carried in the empty room.

"Put your hands over your ears," he called down to her.

"What?"

"Put your hands over your ears!"

"O-okay." She tucked the file folder under one arm and clapped her gloved hands over her ears. About two seconds later, a deep, melodious *bong* tolled through the rock vestibule. The force of the sound made her sway on her feet. She laughed, even as she warned, "You'll shatter the vases in here if you keep that up!"

"I know. Isn't it wonderful?"

It was, really, like standing inside a gigantic bell.

"Come up here and see," he urged.

Glancing around, she laid the folder on the credenza that sat against one wall and tugged off her mittens, tucking them into the pockets of her heavy wool coat, but then she hesitated.

"Robin," he said, just before his face appeared in the open trapdoor above, "come on up. It's perfectly safe." He wore a knit cap and scarf with his coat.

"How did you know it was me?" she asked, moving toward the ladder.

"I recognized your voice, of course."

"Ah."

He reached down a gloved hand as she put a foot on the bottom rung of the wrought iron ladder.

"How does this thing work?"

"It's very simple. There's a tall pole with a hook on one end. I used it to slide open the trap and then to pull down the ladder. When I'm done, I'll use it to push the ladder back up and lift it over the locking mechanism then slide the trap closed."

"I see."

"Oh, you haven't seen anything yet," he told her, grasping her hand and all but lifting her up the last few rungs to stand next to him on a narrow metal platform fixed to one side of the tiny square open-sided belfry. In their bulky coats, they had to stand pressed shoulder to shoulder. "Take a look at this." He swung his arm wide, encompassing the town, the valley beyond and the snowcapped mountains surrounding it all.

"Wow."

"Exactly," he said. "There's a part of Psalm 98 that says, 'Let the rivers clap their hands, let the mountains sing together for joy…' Seeing the view like this, you can almost feel it, can't you? The rivers and mountains praising their creator."

"I never thought of rivers and mountains praising God," she admitted.

"Scripture speaks many times of nature praising God and testifying to His wonders."

"I can see why," she said reverently.

"So can I," he told her, smiling down at her with those warm brown eyes on her face.

Her breath caught in her throat. But she was reading too much into that look. Surely she was reading too much into it. That wasn't appreciation she saw in his gaze. That was just her loneliness seeking connection. Wasn't it? Though she had never felt this sudden, electrical link before, not like this, as if something vital and masculine in him reached out and touched something fundamental and feminine in her, she had to be mistaken.

He was a man of God after all.

Even if she couldn't help thinking of him as just a man.

A shadow seemed to pass behind his brown eyes, as if he'd read her thoughts, and he turned his gaze back to the mountains, visually drinking in snowcapped peaks set against the bright blue sky and the sunshine.

After only a moment, he smiled at her, his genial self again.

Yet Robin felt a distinct chill that she hadn't felt an instant before, a chill that even winter could not explain.

Chapter Two

In an effort to hide her disturbing reaction to Ethan's closeness, Robin turned away from the magnificent sight outside the belfry, leaned back lightly against the hip-high wall and gazed instead at the two bells attached to the crossbeam in front of her. Each of the bells was about as big around as Ethan was, but one was deeper than the other. He stretched out a foot and gave the nearest bell a gentle shove. It rocked to and fro, giving off a delightful peal that, while loud, did not threaten to burst Robin's eardrums or move her bodily, as it had down below. The crossbeam remained steadfast. Had it ever been unsound, it was not now.

Suddenly, the noontime recording played, a trilling carillon, one of several that played every three hours from 9:00 a.m. to 9:00 p.m. daily. It was neither as loud as the sound had been in the chamber below the belfry, nor as rich.

"I did a little research after you called," he told her when the recording stopped. "I was able to find records proving that Silas Massey and his wife not only gave these bells to the church, they had the vestibule and belfry built to accommodate them."

"The rumors that the bells were silenced in resentment

after the Masseys left town were apparently true, then," Robin said, frowning, "but why? Do you suppose it really did have something to do with problems at the bank?"

Ethan shrugged. "All I know is that it's time for these bells to ring again. I'm going to attach some ropes and prepare to use them. Wouldn't it be great to ring these bells for Christmas?"

Robin looked around the small, dusty space. Only the ledge where they stood was wide enough to work from, but he couldn't reach the arm at the top of each bell, where the rope obviously attached, from here. He'd have to crawl along the crosspiece to fix the ropes in place. Meanwhile, the speakers in their wire protective cages sat tucked securely into all four corners, with the recorder that played the bell music presumably housed somewhere safely below.

"Are you sure about this?" she asked. "I love hearing the recorded bells."

"So do I," Ethan admitted, "and we'll still use the recordings for everyday, but for special occasions, we'll have the real bells."

"Real bells would be special," Robin admitted, warily eyeing that crossbeam and the trapdoor open beneath it.

"I'll need your help," he suddenly declared.

"*My* help?" Her gaze shot to his. "Oh, Pastor, I don't know."

"If you help me," he said, "I can attach the ropes with the trap closed. I'm sure there must be a way to safely close the trap from up here, but I haven't figured it out."

"Oh!" She clapped a hand to her chest in relief. "In that case, then yes, I certainly will help you."

"Excellent." He smiled broadly. "Then I won't have to explain about the bells to anyone else. Don't want to start any Massey gossip now that Dale's in town, do we? Not that there's ever a good time to start gossip."

Robin nodded. "I see what you mean."

"I thought you would. Besides, I want this to be a surprise for the congregation. Hopefully, the townsfolk will think any extra bongs they hear around the regular bell times are part of the recordings, so they'll be surprised when I toll the bells for Christmas services," he went on. Then he tugged at his earlobe. "I must think of a way to repay you for all your help."

"You don't have to do that," she said, shaking her head. "Although…"

She worried her bottom lip with her teeth. It was so nice to have someone to talk to. Olivia had become a good friend, but Robin didn't dare trust any of the Jasper Gulch natives with her story. The pastor was an outsider like her, though. Perhaps she should tell him what had brought her to Jasper Gulch and seek his advice on what to do next. On the other hand, what would he think of her once he learned of her duplicity?

"I, um, appreciate you showing me the view from up here," she went on carefully, deciding not to risk it. "It is truly spectacular."

"I'm glad you've enjoyed it," he told her, moving to the ladder, "but that can't be what brought you by this morning."

"No, of course not. I have some photos for you, photos of Christmas decorations from 1913, '14 and '15, a couple from right here in Jasper Gulch. That will give us a good idea of what materials to use, and I also have some websites where we can find instructions on how to replicate the designs."

"We?" he echoed, smiling. "Are you volunteering to help?"

"I'm not a florist or decorator," she hedged. "All I'm trained to do is research."

He grinned and said, "An invaluable help. So what are we waiting for? I'm eager to see what you've brought me."

She watched him disappear through the trapdoor. Only as she stood alone on the tiny platform did she realize how very cold it was up there in the belfry. Even with her coat and scarf on over her slacks and sweater, she shivered, until he called up to her, his voice expanding in the rock room below.

"By the way, I think it's time you started calling me Ethan. Don't you? Lots of the people in town do."

Suddenly she felt warm all over. Would he dare suggest such a thing if he knew that, like all the other unattached women in town, she was quickly forming a crush on the pastor with the warm brown eyes?

Ethan really liked Robin Frazier. He liked her a lot. She had the charming and rare habit of thinking before she spoke. When he'd heard her voice in the vestibule, his heart had rejoiced, for he'd thought of her as he'd gazed out over God's magnificent creation. He'd wished, quite unaccountably, that he could share the vision with her. To have her suddenly appear like that had seemed an answer to a prayer he hadn't dared utter. Or was it?

Ethan had long ago accepted that he would not marry. When he'd taken the pastorate in Jasper Gulch, he'd assumed that the opportunities to marry or even date would be few, but then the matchmaking had begun. Aghast, he'd done his best to hide his disquiet with the situation. Often, he'd felt pursued since coming here and had wished mightily to be left in peace. Still, as those around him had paired off—why, one of the centennial functions had been a wedding ceremony for fifty couples!—he'd felt more and more alone, and he wasn't sure why that should be so. Since the death of his girlfriend, Theresa, he'd had a difficult time even forming friendships with women, let alone romantic attachments.

Until Robin Frazier. Suddenly, he felt as if he'd found

a friend, but it was foolish to even think that he'd found anything more in her. He hardly even knew her! More to the point, she hardly knew him, and if she did, she would almost certainly be appalled. That was one reason he chose not to wear his clerical collar outside the pulpit or when not on official church business. While ignorant of the details, people needed to know that their pastor was a man like any other. In this case, many might find his failings difficult to forgive.

When Ethan had taken over this post, the former pastor had advised that Ethan give himself plenty of time to get established within the community before deciding to share the tragedies and failures of his past. Sometimes Ethan wished he still had Pastor Peters to talk to, but after his retirement Peters had moved to Colorado to be near his daughter and grandchildren, and Ethan didn't feel comfortable imposing on their short acquaintance with chatty telephone calls. As his own family barely spoke to him and his few friends from seminary were all married and busy, Ethan sometimes felt quite alone.

Oh, he'd made friends in Jasper Gulch, but he hadn't found anyone in whom he felt he could confide. What made him think that Robin could be that person? he wondered as Robin crawled gingerly down the ladder.

Quite without meaning to, he found himself guiding her to the bottom, his arms bracketing her slender body, his gloved hands gripping the narrow side rails until her feet safely touched down on the stone floor. Backing away so that she could turn and face him proved surprisingly difficult, which he covered by sweeping off his cap and stuffing it into a coat pocket.

"Let's get the belfry closed so it'll warm up in here."

Grabbing a long pole with two odd hooks on the end, he pushed up the ladder, locked it in place and slid the trapdoor closed.

"That looked easy enough to do," Robin commented.

Ethan nodded as he returned the pole to its corner. It fit snugly into a pair of holders bolted into the rock.

"There's just one thing," she went on, staring up at the closed trapdoor in the rock ceiling. "Where do the ropes come down?"

He lifted a finger and led the way to what had been a deep shelving unit set off to one side of the vestibule. Its twin space on the opposite wall made a tidy coat closet.

"I always thought this was a strange sort of cupboard, recessed as it was with shelves as deep as my arm. When I removed the contents, I found another space with the pulleys and ropes. The ropes themselves are no good, but the wall fittings are all fine. I've already ordered the right type and size of ropes, and they should be here in a week or so.

"I should be able to attach them to the bells. Then all we have to do is hope the bells aren't too badly out of tune to make a pleasant noise for Christmas."

"I didn't know bells could be out of tune."

"Apparently they can, but I think that's when there are several bells involved."

She looked up at the ceiling. "Those two sounded fine to me."

"Do you have musical training?" he asked.

Her clear blue eyes met his, and she touched the mole beneath her eyebrow before calmly saying, "Not much. I sang in glee club in high school and college."

Glee club. He couldn't help thinking that many pastors' wives often had service callings of their own: music, teaching, women's or children's ministry, chaplaincy, even a pastorate of one form or another. He told himself not to be an idiot. All he needed from her was help getting the bells roped and the church decorated.

"I'll let you know when the ropes get here, and we'll set up a time to attach them," he said.

"Sounds like a plan."

"A plan that needs a lot of prayer if it's to succeed," he added with a chortle. "Now, about those pictures you brought with you…"

She went to the credenza that stood against the wall and opened a file folder, spreading out several sheets of paper. Ethan hurried over to take a look. As he studied the pictures she'd brought, he casually unbuttoned his coat.

One photo showed the inside of an unnamed couple's cabin where a small, spindly evergreen tree had been decorated with berries, beads and bits of broken glass. Another showed the front railings of a porch swathed in evergreen boughs. An arrangement of candles and mistletoe on a fireplace mantel with an open Bible and a Christmas postcard was the focus of a third black-and-white photograph.

The final offering had been shot right there in front of the church. It showed the pastor and two others in white smocks with big bows on them, presumably red, and the entire cast of a pageant, including two real sheep, a donkey and, oddly enough, a chicken. Most of the actors were garbed in blankets with lopsided halos and crowns, wings and sashes askew. Most wore cowboy boots beneath their tunics, and one mulish youngster sported his cowboy hat, too, and had a rope slung over one shoulder, despite the shepherd's crook in the other hand. The youngest children all carried chrismon patterns—simple symbols of the Christian faith, such as the shape of a shepherd's crook, dove, Bethlehem star or trumpeting angel. Ethan had to smile.

"Now, *that's* a congregation to keep a pastor on his knees."

"It looks like fun, though, doesn't it?"

"It does. Just look at the smile on the pastor's face."

"I wonder what part the chicken played."

They both laughed over that. Ethan squinted at the tiny type beneath the photo.

"Those are readers in those smocks. They probably read the Christmas story out of the Bible, and the cast acted it out."

"Makes sense."

"We could do something like that," Ethan mused. "That way no one would have to memorize lines."

"I thought you might like to have these, too," she said, offering him several more papers.

"Chrismon patterns."

"They'd be very simple to make out of fabric. And you might want this."

The final sheet contained a list of websites where he could order modern versions of antique Christmas bulbs.

"I think you can find everything else you need out there," she said, waving a hand to indicate the great outdoors. "The various types of greenery have different meanings, you see, and the locals would have been aware of that back then."

"Robin Frazier, you are a gem beyond price. I don't have internet access here, but I can find it. Now, I have just two more questions for you."

"And they are?" she asked cautiously, narrowing her lovely blue eyes at him.

"First, will you serve on the decorating committee?"

She blinked. "Pastor—"

"Ethan," he corrected automatically.

"Ethan," she began again, "I'm not even a member of the church."

"But you are the resident expert on historical Christmas decorations. Or as near as we can come to one."

She bowed her head, smiling. "I see. All right. In that case, of course I'll help out. Just do remember that I have a full-time job."

"Of course. Which leads me to my second question."

"And that is?"

"Are you free on Saturday for gathering greenery?"

"*This* Saturday?"

"It's December 2, Miss Frazier. I'd like to schedule a Hanging of the Green service for a week from tomorrow. We have no time to lose, and you know exactly what sort of greenery people would have gathered a hundred years ago."

She looked around the vestibule before glancing at him once more and nodding.

"Saturday would be fine."

"I'll pick you up about 9:00 a.m., then. If you'll just tell me where you live."

"Oh." Smiling, she lifted a finely boned hand to press a fingertip to that exquisite little mole beneath her eyebrow. "That would help, wouldn't it? I've taken a kitchenette at Fidler's Inn. Room six, on the ground floor."

"Room six," he repeated. "Um, if you have hiking boots, you might want to wear them."

"I can do that."

"And jeans probably wouldn't hurt."

"I can do that, too."

"Okay, then."

She nodded, and they stood there smiling at each other until she suddenly said, "Well, I'd better grab something to eat and get back to work."

"Sure, sure." He cleared his throat, nodding. "Thanks so much for dropping by."

"Thanks for showing me your view."

"Anytime." She started toward the outer door, reaching into her pocket for her gloves, but he called her back. "Uh, Robin. The bell thing. I've told some others that I'm cleaning up the area and doing some research, but I'd really like to keep my plans quiet until Christmas Eve," he reminded her.

"That's fine," she told him. "Whatever you want."

Grinning, he couldn't resist ribbing her a little. "Whatever I want, eh?"

"Within reason," she retorted through a smile.

"I'm a very reasonable man," he said, straight-faced.

"What you are, Pastor Ethan Johnson," she said, shaking a dainty finger at him, "is a tease."

"Maybe a little bit," he admitted, smiling, "at least with you. It's just that you're so very serious. Sweet but serious." And he should learn to keep his mouth shut. Her blue gaze clouded and skidded away.

Long seconds ticked by before she said, "I have to go."

He followed her to the door, wondering if he shouldn't enlist someone else to help gather the greenery and knowing he wouldn't. "Goodbye, Robin."

"Goodbye, Ethan," she whispered. He'd have missed it if the acoustics in the room hadn't been so extraordinary.

She pushed out into the December sunshine. He followed, calling after her as her footsteps fell swiftly across the plank walkway, "Nine o'clock, Saturday. Don't forget."

"I won't."

He watched her walk away, wondering if God was telling him that the past could finally be put away once and for all. Or had he come to Jasper Gulch to make another hideous mistake?

Robin did not next see Ethan Johnson on Saturday as she assumed she would; she saw him on Thursday evening. He called that day to say that he'd put together a committee to plan, design and construct decorations for the church, but because the ladies felt they hadn't a minute to lose, they wanted to meet that night. What could she say, that she'd rather not see him again so soon because she found him entirely too attractive for her peace of mind? Of course, she said that she would attend the meeting, and then she prayed for some way to get out of it.

While she was mentally sorting through excuses, her landlady, Mamie Fidler, stopped by her room to say that she was on the committee, too, and going to the meeting.

"Might as well head over there together. No sense in both of us burning gasoline."

Sixtyish, single and no-nonsense, Mamie Fidler wore hiking boots, denim skirts and flannel shirts year-round everywhere she went, even to church. She had "decorated" the Fidler Inn with utilitarian hominess, so Robin was somewhat surprised that Ethan had recruited her for the committee. On the other hand, Mamie was handy with all sorts of tools, including fishing poles and skinning knives, and she was brutally efficient.

"I'll drive," Robin volunteered.

"I'll get my gear. You got a slicker?"

"I'm afraid not."

"Too bad," Mamie opined, shaking her head.

That was how Robin found herself rushing through a light but wet snowfall in twenty-degree weather over a boardwalk dusted with a mixture of rock salt and sand toward a rectangle of light in the darkness. The door in the education wing of the building opened well before they reached it, and Ethan rushed out, armed with an umbrella. Mamie, covered head to ankle in a shapeless water-repellent poncho, plowed ahead, disappearing into the hallway.

"I'm so sorry," Ethan told Robin, shaking off the umbrella before collapsing it and pulling it in behind them so he could close the door. "The skies were gray earlier, but the weather forecast didn't call for snow."

"The weather bureau should consult Mamie."

"I'm sure that's true," he agreed with a chuckle. "I find

it wise to consult Mamie on a lot of things, like where's the best place to find the greenery we'll need and how to keep it from drying out too badly before Christmas comes."

Ah. Now things were making sense. "You're a wise man."

He laughed. "Maintain that thought, will you?" Placing his warm hand at the small of her back, he applied light pressure, saying softly, "Come along and meet the others, but be forewarned. Some here are used to taking charge in every situation. In this, however, *you* are our guide. Understand?"

She nodded absently. Even through the thickness of her coat, his touch unsettled her, so she set about nonchalantly peeling off the outer garment as they walked through the corridor to the meeting room. As soon as they reached their destination, he offered to take her things and stow them on a table with everyone else's. Familiar faces turned from a second table set with muffins and a Crock-Pot of apple cider.

In addition to Mamie Fidler, Robin recognized Allison Douglas, Rosemary Middleton and her daughter, Marie, Abigail Rose and Nadine Shaw, the mayor's wife. Everyone greeted Robin and invited her to partake of the muffins, provided by Rosemary, who ran the local grocery along with her husband, and cider, which Allison had brought. Marie Middleton would be of great use, being a florist. Nadine's inclusion made sense because her eldest daughter, Faith, was marrying Dale Massey on Christmas night, so the decorations would be of special interest to her, but Robin couldn't help feeling nervous around any of the Shaws, the mayor and his wife in particular.

Robin made a point of sitting at the opposite end of the conference table from Nadine, and unless it was her imagination, Ethan made a point of sitting next to her. Everyone else seemed to think so, too, though Abigail was the only one who gave an overt sign, raising both eyebrows. The others merely traded casual glances, all except Mamie, but Robin knew her landlady well enough by now not to mistake the twinkle in her golden eyes.

Ethan's attention was explained when he raised his head from the opening prayer and said, "Now, then, ladies, thanks to Robin, you have before you copies of photos of Christmas decorations from one hundred years ago." He went on to say that she had agreed to act as their historical consultant on this project. That won her smiles from the others, and she relaxed somewhat. "Robin," he concluded firmly, "will have the final say on all designs."

Soon they were all deep in conversation about swags, garlands and wreaths, as well as the past tendency to attach meanings to certain types of greenery. Marie started sketching, and Mamie set about estimating the necessary foot length of boughs that would be needed. Before long they had a design and a plan. Nadine divided up the responsibilities, and everyone went along without protest until she came to gathering the greenery itself.

"We'll take care of that on the Shaw Ranch."

"Uh, no, we have that covered already," Ethan said.

"But—"

"The McGuire Ranch has more of what we need," Mamie stated bluntly.

"You have enough to worry about," Allison pointed out, "with the wedding and all."

"Robin and I will take care of the greenery," Ethan insisted, looping an arm around the back of Robin's chair.

Just like that, every eye riveted to the pair of them again, and just like that, Robin's breath caught in her throat.

"We, um, want to leave you and Marie free to concentrate on the wedding," she offered with a wan smile.

"And I need Robin's expertise on the specific meanings of the various types of greenery," Ethan said. The speculation in the eyes around the table did not dim one iota, however.

"Who would really know the difference these days?" Nadine asked.

"I would," he answered firmly, and that was the end of it.

Robin wondered if Ethan realized that he had just made them the object of conjecture and gossip. Surely he wouldn't want that, especially if he ever found out why she'd really come to town. A pastor wouldn't want to be linked to a woman who had come here under false pretenses to meet the family who didn't even know she existed.

Then again, perhaps she had misjudged him entirely and he would be all too glad for a connection, any connection, no matter how distant, to the first family of Jasper Gulch—that was, if the Shaws didn't toss her out on her ear the instant they discovered the truth about her great-grandmother Lillian.

Or rather, Lucy.

Chapter Three

It occurred to Ethan, belatedly, that the speculation about him and Robin Frazier could serve a purpose. He hadn't meant to suggest that a romance might be brewing between then, but the presence of a possible love interest could provide him with a shield against unwanted attention. Perhaps, if everyone thought his own interest to be fixed, he could relax, at least for a little while, instead of being on constant alert for lures being cast his way.

The thought buoyed the young pastor so much that within hours the next morning, he had women sewing chrismon symbols out of white fabric and nearly a dozen children lined up for parts in the Christmas pageant to be performed on Christmas Eve. Moreover, he was busy writing a script, dependent largely on scripture, for the reading, which he proposed to do with one man and two women.

He was surprised by how quickly the whole program began to take shape in his mind. He didn't imagine that Christmas-pageant costuming had actually changed much across the centuries since the time of Christ, but he wanted to copy what had been used in Jasper Gulch one hundred years ago, and he would require Robin's help to ensure accuracy. Before even that, however, he suddenly found himself in need of some expert advice on historical Hanging of the Green services.

It was an old tradition of mostly European origin, and he'd been through several of them, but he wanted this year's service to be as authentic as possible as one that might have taken place a hundred years ago in Jasper Gulch. So off to the museum he went on Friday. He stopped off at the diner and picked up a sandwich on the way, arriving close to the lunch hour. Leaving the half-eaten sandwich in the cold car, he went in to find Robin and Olivia sharing brown-bagged meals in the break room.

"Ethan!" Olivia greeted him, smiling broadly over the rim of a steaming cup of soup. Like Robin, she didn't look much older than a teen, with her petite stature, blond hair and sparkling blue eyes. She'd married Jack McGuire in October at the centennial's Old Tyme Wedding, to no one's real surprise. The two had a well-known history that had made them an item from the moment Olivia had stepped foot back into town after an absence of several years. "Jack tells me that you're coming out Saturday to raid the place for greenery."

He shot a glance at Robin, who sat staring at a prepackaged potpie on which she'd barely broken the crust. "Yes. Um, Mamie Fidler judges that the McGuire Ranch has the greatest variety of greenery hereabouts."

"She's right," Olivia said, stirring her soup. "There's cedar, which symbolizes royalty, fir and pine for everlasting life, holly, which represents the ultimate mission of Christ on the cross, and ivy, a symbol of resurrection. All would have been well known, I imagine, to anyone halfway versed in the traditions of the church a hundred years ago."

"More so than today, it would seem," Ethan muttered.

"Don't forget the bells," Robin put in. "Bells to signify the birth of royalty."

Ethan shared a conspiratorial smile with her as Olivia said, "And I thought jingle bells were just for fun."

He cleared his throat and mused, "Obviously, you two have already done excellent research." He looked to Robin then and added, "I don't suppose we could find an order of service or program for the Hanging of the Green ceremony, could we?"

She didn't even have to think it over. "From a hundred years ago? Doubtful. If such a thing exists, it would be in your files."

He shook his head. "There's nothing there. At least not that I can find."

"We might find something online from another church in another part of the country, if that will be of help to you."

"I suppose it'll have to do. I did think of it, but surfing the internet on my cell phone is not very handy."

"I'll take a look for you," Robin said, starting to rise.

Ethan waved her back down into her chair. "Finish your lunch first. It can wait."

"Maybe you'd like to join us," Olivia offered. "I could heat you a cup of soup in the microwave."

"Well," he said, smiling, "if you're sure. I just happen to have a sandwich in the car." With the temperature hovering just above freezing, he'd judged that the sandwich would be as safe in his car as in a refrigerator.

"Your soup will be ready when you return," Robin promised, getting to her feet, "and my pie should be cool enough to eat by then, too."

"In that case, I'll be glad to join you," he told her, setting off.

He caught the speculative look that Olivia sent Robin as he slipped back out into the hallway. He felt a pang of guilt about that, but that was how it went in a small town, or so he told himself.

* * *

Strangely, while Ethan was at the museum sharing lunch with her and Olivia in the break room, Robin looked forward to Saturday's outing with him. Later, as he sat at her shoulder while she searched the internet for historically accurate Hanging of the Green services, she couldn't help being intensely aware of his every breath, murmur and movement with a kind of joyous expectation. Later, they surfed the web looking for and ordering delicate, period-appropriate glass bulbs and electric candles, as real ones would be too dangerous to use. Only after he went on his way, leaving her to her usual work, did she begin to have serious doubts about keeping company with him.

Perhaps the speculative looks that Olivia slid her way when she thought Robin wasn't looking were to blame. Or maybe it was realizing how much she was coming to enjoy the pastor's easy company. The phone call that she received as she was letting herself into her room at the Fidler Inn that evening certainly didn't help.

"Hello," she said, juggling her things. "One minute, please."

"Robin?"

The sound of her mother's voice instantly made the industrial carpet seem a more dull shade of brown than usual, and the creamy faux chinking between the faux logs on the walls suddenly became a rather uninspiring tan.

"Robin, is that you?"

"Yes, of course, Mother. Who else would it be?"

Her kitchen, which consisted of a six-foot length of brown cabinet that held a two-burner stovetop, a tiny microwave, minifridge, bar sink and four-cup coffeemaker, had been entirely adequate before; yet now she saw it as ridiculously lacking, even for a single woman whose main meals were prepackaged and microwaved.

"Well, it could be anyone, for all I know," Sheila Frazier complained. "It's been days since we last spoke, and you might have moved out of that dreadful motel by now."

Strange. Ethan had recognized her voice after a single chance meeting. Well, perhaps more than one. But shouldn't her own mother be able to recognize her voice? And how did Sheila know what the inn was like? She'd never been here. Still, the comfy patchwork quilt on the bed suddenly seemed faded and old, and the unstained woodwork that had struck Robin as so fresh when she'd first come to stay at the Fidler Inn now appeared unfinished, incomplete.

Dropping her handbag on the bed, Robin stared at the little square dining table—which bore no resemblance to the pair of chairs that flanked it—and steeled herself for the conversation to come, her mood shifting just as her surroundings had.

Sighing, she asked, "What is it, Mother?"

"I thought you should know that a position has come open as a research assistant here at the university. The Templeton foundation is endowing the position, so if you apply, you're guaranteed to get it. I know it smacks of nepotism, but after all the good the Templetons have done the university, we are not ashamed to—"

"Mother," Robin interrupted, wondering why she couldn't exercise the same circumspection with her own family that she did with everyone else, "this position is in the science department, isn't it?"

"Well, of course, but you are a trained and able researcher."

"I am a historian," Robin said, enunciating each syllable clearly, her temper barely in check. "I know you place no value on that, but history is what I love. History is what I do. And I already have a job as a historian here in Jasper Gulch." Never mind that it barely paid above minimum wage or that she'd been thinking of leaving.

Her mother's reply was exactly what Robin expected.

"Oh, honestly. You cannot mean to bury yourself in that hideous little throwback of a town, where you don't even have decent cell-phone service so I have to call you at your *motel,* all in the vain hopes of connecting with some jumped-up cowpokes who just happen to be distant relatives."

Robin pinched the bridge of her nose. "Mother, do you not realize that you are displaying the very same attitude that drove Great-Grandma Lillian away from her home?"

"And you are determined to follow in her footsteps!" Sheila Templeton Frazier, Ph.D., insisted shrilly. "What have we done that is so awful?"

"You haven't done anything, Mother," Robin said. "I didn't come here to get away from you. I came in search of something more. Why won't you listen?"

"And why won't you understand," Sheila countered, "that you are nothing to these Shaws? You will never be anything to them but a lying little opportunist, Robin. You may think that because they've accepted young Massey into the fold, they'll accept you, too, if only for the Templeton name, but I assure you that is not the case. Even if they believe your claims, which I doubt, once they understand that Templeton funds are tied up exclusively in the foundation for scientific research, they'll bar you from the door. Mark my words. How many times has it happened before?"

Sadly, Robin had lost more than one erstwhile friend who, having discovered her Templeton relationship, had thought she could command the Templeton money. Only those connected with the Templeton Foundation for Scientific Research enjoyed the largesse of Templeton funds, however, and Robin had long ago decided that science was not her calling. Her father managed the foundation, from which her Templeton grandparents had both retired. Her mother was herself a research scientist, so the Templeton foundation was, in a very real sense, the family business. But not—much to the chagrin of her parents—for Robin.

She was fully aware that if she didn't somehow engage with the foundation or marry someone who could be taken into the foundation, all the Templeton money would pass out of the family's control with the deaths of her parents. And that was fine with her. What the Templetons didn't seem to understand was that family was more important to Robin than foundations or money. They just didn't understand how sad and lonely she was because her acknowledged family consisted of only her parents, her Templeton grandparents and one unmarried Frazier uncle, her father's brother, Richard, none of whom seemed to value her in any real way. They looked down on her profession. They looked down on her relationship with her beloved late great-grandmother. They even looked down on her faith, which she'd learned at her great-grandma's knee.

She'd never known her Gillette grandparents. Her Frazier grandparents had both died when she was young; she didn't even remember her grandmother, Dorothy Elaine Gillette Frazier. Perhaps that was why she had been so close to her great-grandmother, Lillian Gillette. And that was why, a year after her beloved great-grandma's death, she had come here to Montana to find what remained of her family. Her Shaw family. Lillian, many would be shocked to know, was not Lillian at all but rather Lucy Shaw, whom entire generations of Shaws thought dead and buried for decades.

They all assumed that Lucy Shaw had died in 1926 when her Model T automobile had careened off the Beaver Creek Bridge into the rushing water below. They had no idea that Robin's great-grandma Lillian had confessed on her deathbed, at the ripe old age of one hundred and three, that she was Lucy Shaw and had faked her own death in

order to run away from Montana to New Mexico with her
beloved Cyrus. Lillian—or Lucy, rather—had encouraged
her lonely great-granddaughter to find her Shaw relatives
in Montana, but Robin's father and mother had insisted
that Lillian had been raving when she'd come up with the
"Montana story."

Several weeks ago, Robin had finally found enough
proof to convince her that Lillian's story was true. Lillian was Lucy, but Robin's parents wanted nothing to do
with the Shaws, considering them little more than country
bumpkins who would try to impose on the storied Templeton name and the science foundation that her mother's
family and Robin's father so assiduously protected.

Sadly, as her parents had recently pointed out, Robin
now had little reason to believe that the Shaws would want
to have anything to do with her. After all, she had been
living and working among them under false pretenses for
months. Her parents wanted her to forget the Shaws and
come home to New Mexico to "do something useful" with
her life, the study of history not being on their list of useful endeavors.

If only Robin had trusted Great-Grandma Lillian and
not let her parents put doubts into her head about the veracity of Lillian's story, she wouldn't be in such a mess now.
She could have gone to the Shaws with a straightforward
story and looked for proof without subterfuge, but she'd
been so afraid of branding her beloved great-grandmother
a liar that she'd become a liar herself. Even though she'd
found the proof she'd sought, her mother was right that
the Shaws weren't likely to look kindly upon her lies. And
neither, she imagined, would Ethan Johnson. What man
of God would?

So, despite her brave words to her mother over the
phone, Robin worried that she ought not to accompany
Ethan the next morning. After the call ended, she hung

up the bedside phone and sat brooding about it for several minutes.

She sensed that Ethan was a very special man and that under other circumstances something special might even develop between them, but her deceit had surely doomed any possible relationship already. It would, she was convinced, be better simply to end her association with him entirely. Perhaps she ought to just leave Jasper Gulch altogether. Maybe her mother's phone call was a sign of that. Maybe God was trying to tell her to get out now before she humiliated herself.

When the phone rang, her cell phone this time, she halfway expected it to be Ethan telling her that he wouldn't need her assistance on Saturday after all.

Instead, he said, "I'm making a terrible pest of myself, aren't I?"

She had to laugh. "Hello to you, too, Ethan."

"Oh, good. She's not ready to hang up on me. Yet."

Smiling, she rolled her eyes. "What is it now?"

The phone crackled, as cell phones tended to do in Jasper Gulch, then he very clearly said, "Would it be a terrible imposition if I asked you to come to the church this evening? I need some advice concerning the pageant."

She held her breath, wondering if she ought to refuse simply because she so very much wanted to see him.

After a moment, he softly counseled, "You know, it's okay to pray about these things first. I do."

She touched her eyebrow and closed her eyes, picturing him with that phone in his hand, praying about whether or not to call her, but then she shook her head. That wasn't what he meant. Surely that wasn't what he meant.

"What time?"

"Around seven?"

"Seven it is."

"Great." She could hear the relief in his voice. "Weather

shouldn't be a problem, but dress warmly. The sanctuary
is chilly on a Friday evening."

"All right."

"See you soon."

She broke the connection and sighed. Whatever was
wrong with her? Did she have to go looking for a broken
heart? Maybe she should just tell him that she couldn't
go with him tomorrow and put an end to this whole silly
crush before she did something truly stupid.

She turned up at seven sharp, her pale gold hair twisted
into a prim knot atop her head. It seemed to Ethan that
she'd come armored, with a wide headband that covered
her ears and a big, fuzzy, shapeless pale green sweater that
covered her almost from knees to chin. Brown leggings
and half boots completed the ensemble. She looked rather
like a prickly pear, and he had to wonder if that was the
point, so wary did she seem at first.

He'd felt compelled to call her. Indeed, seeing her tonight had seemed absolutely imperative. Nevertheless, he
welcomed her skittishness and got right down to business,
leading her straight into the sanctuary to describe in detail
his ideas for the Christmas Eve pageant.

"What do you think?" he asked, finally winding down.
"Now, I know they wouldn't have had this great space to
work with, so I'm open to suggestions."

Robin walked back and forth, considering carefully before saying, "We could put down a tarp and scatter some
hay, maybe stack up a few bales and cover them with hopsacking."

"Very doable."

"We could also paint a backdrop and string it up on
rope."

"Which do you think would be more in keeping with
the period?" Ethan asked.

She tilted her head, thinking it over, perhaps picturing it. "I think we should use loose hay and build a rough stable with timbers or logs."

"I agree. I'll get some of the men on it, but I'll need you to approve their plans. If you don't mind."

She clasped her hands behind her back and, after a moment, shrugged. He let out a silent breath.

"About the costumes," she suddenly began, "the fabrics will be the important part. I'll ask around. Maybe Mamie has some vintage stuff. If not, we'll have to arrange a trip into Bozeman or another larger town."

A smile broke across his face. "Thank you. I couldn't do this without you, any of it."

To his utter relief, she smiled. "Glad to be of service."

He laughed, feeling tons lighter, and impulsively took her hand in his, saying, "I will be so relieved when we have all the greenery gathered."

Frowning, she pulled her hand free and turned away. Ethan's heart abruptly sank.

"Robin, is everything okay?"

She sent him a quick, joyless smile. "Oh, you know how it is. Christmas can be a bittersweet time."

"Are you missing your family?"

She turned to face him then looked down at her toes. "Yes and no. Sadly, I don't miss the family I have, but I do miss the family I don't have. Strange, isn't it?"

"I'm not sure I follow you," he admitted.

"You couldn't," she told him with a shake of her head. "But we ought to miss family, don't you think?"

"Yes," he said simply, "but family is sometimes a burden."

Her round, blue gaze sharpened. "Is yours?"

He wanted to tell her then, everything, about his losses and disappointments, his fears and heartbreaks, his hopes and needs, but he didn't dare.

"Some of them are," he answered evasively. "I miss my sister and niece, though."

"Oh? Will they come for Christmas?"

Sadness stabbed him. "I doubt it." That was a half-truth at best, though, and he suddenly wanted very much to give Robin better, so he followed it with a flat "No."

For some reason, she seemed almost as disappointed as he felt. "That's too bad."

"Will your family come here for Christmas?" he asked.

She didn't even pause to think. "Oh, no. They wouldn't."

"Will you go there?" It hadn't occurred to him until that very moment that she might, and he suddenly realized that all his plans would crumble without her.

As was her custom, she mulled over her answer for a moment, but then she shook her head. "No, I won't go there."

Ethan didn't try to hide his relief. He let it beam out of him. "I am selfishly glad. I don't think I could pull off this centennial Christmas without your help, and I wouldn't want to try."

She smiled then, genuinely smiled. He clasped his hands behind his back, the sudden need to reach out and pull her against him shaking him to his toes. Instead, he offered to walk her to her car. It was the gentlemanly thing to do, after all, though he was having some trouble with the gentlemanly thing at the moment.

As she drove away into the night, he prayed for guidance. And self-control. It had been a very long time since he'd felt anything like what Robin Frazier stirred in him.

For a moment, long-dormant memory swamped him. Suddenly he was back in Los Angeles, standing on the curb in broad daylight, Theresa beside him. He heard the squeal of tires and the sharp, rapid staccato of gunshots. He felt himself flinch and throw up his arms, dropping to his knees as dust and bits of concrete stung his skin, and then as abruptly as it had begun, it was over, except that almost at once the iron-rich smell of blood rose into his nostrils, coating the back of his throat. He opened his eyes to find Theresa on her back with her dark hair spread across the sidewalk, her arms flung haphazardly across her slender body, a neat hole in her forehead and another in her neck, her dark eyes wide but unseeing, as he tried in his panic to keep her from leaving him. Some part of him had known from the first glimpse that she was already gone, but he'd had to try.

He hadn't tried to hold a woman since then, and he never meant to.

"Ah, Lord," he whispered, "don't let me go back there. Give me courage, wisdom and guidance, the strength to realize all that You plan for me and to walk away from anything that is not Your will. Anything and anyone."

No matter how compelling.

Chapter Four

Somehow, when Robin was with Ethan, she felt strangely disconnected from the pitfalls that surrounded her. She knew intellectually that any relationship around Jasper Gulch was potentially problematic for her. As soon as her deceptions were discovered, people were bound to choose sides, and most would undoubtedly side against her and with the Shaws. Still, Ethan's very presence tended to make her awareness of that fact fade into the background. That was part of what made him so dangerous.

As soon as they parted company, however, her thoughts would begin to seethe with very reasonable doubts and fears. She would quite naturally recall that her position in Jasper Gulch was tenuous at best, even with Ethan himself, perhaps *especially* with Ethan. No minister would look kindly at a woman who had come into a community under false pretenses and perpetuated the lie for months on end. That being the case, she wondered again if she should go on seeing Ethan. He seemed to addle her thought processes and blunt some of her emotions while exciting others.

Recalling that Ethan had told her to pray about things before she made a decision, Robin prayed that night, asking for clarity and wisdom. Exhausted, she fell asleep, assuming that God had essentially told her to leave Jasper Gulch, the Shaws and Ethan Johnson behind. Yet, when she woke in the morning, she found that she had just enough time to dress before the young pastor arrived to pick her up—and no time to arrange for anyone else to accompany him on his mission. Then Mamie showed up at her door with a pair of sturdy work gloves, snowshoes, a small handsaw and a plate of hot, melt-in-your-mouth cinnamon rolls about three inches thick to combat the cold air that she let in with her.

What else could Robin do but hurriedly dress and wolf down cinnamon rolls while coffee percolated and Mamie made the bed? Ethan showed up while Mamie and Robin were demolishing the third of four monster cinnamon rolls and happily helped himself to the last one.

"Just think," he quipped, "I'm keeping you both from the sin of gluttony, and at detriment to my own soul, too, as I came here from breakfast at Great Gulch Grub."

They all laughed, then Robin confessed, "You might have kept Mamie from the sin of gluttony, but not me. I've already eaten way too much."

"That makes two of us, then," he said, mopping the icing from the plate with his finger. "Guess we'd better get out there and work it off."

She finished her coffee, enjoying the bite of the black brew juxtaposed against the sweetness of Mamie's cinnamon rolls, then rinsed the cup, gathered her things and went out into the cold, leaving Mamie to lock up behind them. God, Robin supposed, didn't mean for her to leave Jasper Gulch right away after all. Otherwise, would He have allowed her this feeling of sweet, joyous anticipation after her long night of doubts?

They drove out to the McGuire's Double M Ranch in Ethan's old car because it had all-wheel drive, which he said had come in quite handy, given that some of his congregation lived as far as forty miles outside town. He played music through his smartphone connection along the way, and Robin found herself singing along with some of her favorite praise songs and hymns.

He smiled at her from time to time and once said, "You're more accomplished than you let on."

She shook her head. "No, not really. I don't have much range or resonance. I really can only sing in groups."

"Nothing wrong with that."

"I suppose."

As they drew near the new sprawling house with its blue metal roof and deep porches, Jack and Olivia came out to meet them. Both wore nothing more than their shirtsleeves, though Olivia had pulled the cuffs of her sweater down over her hands. The twenty-eight-degree weather didn't seem to faze them a bit. Guess that came from being natives to the area. When Robin and Ethan got out of the car, Jack leaned a shoulder against the porch support and looked up at the sky, a uniform shade of pale gray today.

"Mornin', Ethan, Robin. Good day for you. Temperature ought to top out above freezing."

Bundled up like a polar bear, Robin smiled wanly. She supposed thirty-three was, technically, above freezing.

"You're going to have to go upslope, though, to find some of the firs," Olivia pointed out. "We have snowshoes if you need them."

"We came prepared," Ethan assured her.

Olivia waved at the ATV parked in front of the house. Every one of the ranchers in the area seemed to have the all-terrain vehicles, and old-timer Rusty Zidek, who was well into his nineties, sometimes used one to get around town even now. Except for the color, this one reminded Robin of Rusty's. Bright yellow and designed for two people to ride side by side with a flatbed behind, it resembled a small, stripped-down version of an early Jeep. A tiny wagon had been attached for good measure.

"Are you sure you don't want us to go with you?" Olivia asked. "This is a big place, you could get lost out here."

"It's all planned out, hon," Jack assured her. "Ethan and I have gone over it in detail. He's got GPS, an aerial map in case of weak signal and detailed instructions. They'll be fine. Besides, they're just going up as far as Gazebo, where they'll eat lunch, and then on to Whistler. They should be back here by two." He looked to Ethan then and said, "If you're not here by half past, I come looking for you."

Ethan nodded and answered, "Understood."

Olivia, meanwhile, was smiling at Robin. "Gazebo," she said, as if that had some special meaning. "I see. Well, then, don't let us keep you."

Ethan started transferring their gear, which included an odd sort of cooler, to the flatbed of the ATV. They climbed in, buckled up and were off. The thing proved to be a surprisingly loud form of transportation. Robin was thankful that Mamie had insisted she take a knit headband to wear under the hood of her coat, and not just because the cold wind would have sliced off her ears. And to think that it was only the sixth day of December.

Winters in Albuquerque and Santa Fe could be cold, but the lows there approximated the averages here, and with three hundred–plus days of sunshine and low humidity year-round, Robin had barely noticed the change of seasons back in New Mexico. Here the seasons were distinct, the precipitation and humidity overwhelming for a desert rat such as herself and winter seemed to be gray more often than not. And the storms! Last month's freak winter storm and the resulting power outage had frightened Robin. If not for Mamie and her backup generator, Robin wasn't sure what she'd have done. Even then, warm bathwater had been scarce.

Now here she was setting off into what amounted to wilderness with none other than the pastor at her side, and unless she was mistaken, he didn't have any more experience at this kind of thing than she did. They were well out of sight of the house when he stopped the ATV at a splintered wood post and consulted both the GPS and the aerial map that he took out of his coat pocket and unfolded across the interior of the small vehicle. It felt amazingly warm once they stopped moving. He showed her exactly where they were on the map, and she felt better, knowing that he was on top of things.

"What's the deal about Gazebo?" she asked as he refolded the map.

"I don't think it's a real gazebo," Ethan said, "just a kind of shelter that Jack's parents put up to protect a picnic table in a spot where they could look down on the valley and their home. Jack suggested it as a good place for us to have lunch."

"I see. I didn't think about lunch."

"I did," Ethan told her with a subtle smile.

Did he ever. Another fifteen minutes took them up the mountain on the west side of the valley high enough for them to find the kind of evergreen growth they needed. Robin had brought photos with her, so they were able to identify the cedar, pine and fir they wanted. Much of it they were able to cut with simple pruning shears, but the larger boughs required the saws.

They needed the snowshoes only once, when they went after a particular pine. Most of the trees were too tall for them to reach the branches, but the trees were smaller at the higher elevations, where the snow tended to pile up and stay around. It was up near Gazebo where they spotted the accessible pine, and they had to hike up to get it. They practically denuded the poor thing, taking two trips to get the fragrant boughs down.

"Why don't I go up with the net and bring down the last load alone while you set the table for lunch," he proposed.

"Great," she agreed. "I know I pigged out at breakfast, but I'm so hungry now I think I could eat a bear."

He laughed, and no wonder, for that was just about what he'd packed. She peeked into the strange, foil-lined "cooler" and found containers of hot vegetable soup, toasty melted-cheese sandwiches, warm ham-and-pea salad, fat rolls stuffed with sausages, a hash-brown potato casserole and thick slabs of brownie cake covered with melted chocolate and broken walnuts. She left it all in the steamy warmer and instead raided the box he'd brought along for a flannel-lined vinyl tablecloth, matching checked cloth napkins, dinnerware, flatware and cups for the coffee he'd included. She warmed herself with that until he returned, gazing at the valley below and the homey two-story ranch house in the distance where Mick McGuire and his new family lived.

Sheltered by the trees and the roof, the gazebo felt, if not warm, at least survivable, especially with the warm coffee inside her and the bounty of Ethan's picnic at her elbow. Ethan arrived a few moments later, tugged off his gloves and straddled the wood bench beside her.

"It's beautiful, isn't it?"

"Oh, yes."

"So different from Los Angeles."

"And New Mexico."

"God must take real pleasure in His creation, just the variety and bounty of it," Ethan said. "No place I've ever been makes me want to worship more than Montana, though."

"That's a lovely way of putting it."

"It's a lovely feeling." He looked her straight in the eye when he said that.

All the world seemed to pause in that moment. She felt his words to her bones. She let them settle into her. She thought of all the sermons she'd every heard, all the words of wisdom she'd ever read, but none of them had ever moved her or touched her as deeply as Ethan's simple declaration.

He loved it here. He had been called here to this place, to serve his Lord and these people. She envied him that calling, that belonging. She admired him for it.

He turned his bare hands palms up and asked, "Will you pray with me before we eat?"

She set aside her mug, tugged off her gloves and placed her hands in his, her head bowed and her heart aquiver.

They enjoyed a sumptuous meal.

"As sumptuous as Great Gulch Grub can make it," Ethan told Robin with a chuckle.

"It was good of you to think of lunch."

"Men always think of their stomachs," he said with a wink. He had to stop that. For some reason he felt compelled to flirt with her. It was immature and foolish and had to stop.

She looked down shyly, scraping a fingertip across the checked vinyl of the tablecloth. "I'm surprised they put in a real tablecloth and napkins."

"Oh, no, that was me," he said without thinking, and her blue eyes zipped up in surprise. "Uh, Jack mentioned that the tabletop was rough planking, and I didn't want to take a chance on paper napkins blowing away," he finished lamely, letting the words dwindle into silence, only to have her beam at him.

"That was very sweet of you."

"It's just a tablecloth and napkins," he said, ridiculously pleased.

They packed up and set off to Whistler, a notch in the rock where the wind was said to make high-pitched noises from time to time, in search of holly. Sure enough, just as Jack had said, they found several basketball-size clumps growing out of crevices in the sheer rock face. All were too far up to easily reach, however. Ethan thought a moment and came up with a plan.

"You could sit on my shoulder," he proposed, "and use those long-handled pruning shears to cut the holly at the base."

She touched her eyebrow. "And if I drop the shears on your head?"

"I'll try not to drop you, too."

She rolled her eyes, even as she reached for the shears with one hand. Ethan went down on one knee, and she climbed up, settling her weight onto his right shoulder.

"Ready?" he asked, wrapping both arms around her knees.

"I guess."

"Up we go, then." He stood. She weighed…just what she should. If he hadn't needed to hold his head at a somewhat awkward angle, he could have carried her for some distance like this. As it was, he only had to walk a few steps to the rock face. She reached above her and, with some effort, clipped off the first clump, which fell right down into his face.

"Sorry!"

He spit specks of dirt out of his mouth, eyes blinking rapidly. "My fault. From now on, I'll look down."

"Can you move sideways a couple feet?"

Stepping over the big clump of holly, he moved to his left. This time, she used the shears to flick the clump behind them.

"Good job."

"Think I have a future as a holly harvester?" she joked, stretching to get another big ball.

He assisted by lifting her slightly, heaving her up by the knees. "I think you have a future as anything God ordains."

"Walked into that one, didn't I?" she quipped, managing the third clump. "One more."

She wound up basically standing in his hands, against the rock wall, to reach the final ball of holly. After it fell, she dropped the shears well away from him. "You can let me down now."

"If you insist," he told her playfully, backing up a step so she could bend her knees and resume her place on his shoulder.

His arms were shaking a bit by the time she was safely seated again, but he was feeling quite powerful and manly—and glad that he'd been working out regularly with the weights in his basement. Showing off a bit, he reached up to grasp her about the waist and twirl her to face him, almost dropping her in the process. Instantly, he clamped his arms around her and felt her body slam into his, knocking the breath from both of them. When his vision cleared, they were standing wrapped in each other's arms, her face turned up to his. It took a supreme act of will, bolstered by a silent prayer, to drop his arms and step back.

"Oops," he managed to say, putting on what was undoubtedly a goofy smile.

"No harm done," she chirped gaily, whipping around to begin gathering up the great clumps of holly.

Ethan sincerely hoped some of it was usable. And that his heart, which was climbing into his throat, didn't strangle him. He had very nearly kissed the woman.

Pastor, he told himself sternly, *get hold of your unruly self.*

Now, if only his unruly self would listen.

"Gazebo," Olivia purred into Robin's ear while the guys shifted the greenery, along with the tree they'd cut, and gear from the ATV into and onto Ethan's Subaru at the McGuire ranch house. "So how was it?"

"Cold," Robin answered nonchalantly, lest her friend make more of the meal than she should. "The food was good, though."

"You know the significance of that spot, don't you?"

Robin shrugged. "Ethan said something about Jack's parents going up there to gaze out across their property."

"Gaze across their property, my eye. Oh, it does have a pretty view, all right. They used to camp up there. A lot. To get away. You know, for privacy. According to Jack, they called it their 'spooning spot.'"

Robin felt her cheeks heat, but she was saved the difficulty of making a reply when Ethan closed the tailgate of the car and announced that they had to get going.

"Ethan says they have to get back to town," Jack told Olivia, as if warning her not to protest, "and you've been outside without your coat too long, Livvie McGuire."

Olivia made a face, but she scampered to the warmth of her husband's side, snuggling beneath his arm, and waved goodbye as Robin all but dived into the passenger seat of the car.

"I hope you don't mind," Ethan said, dropping down behind the steering wheel. "I promised the ladies they could get started on the decorations this afternoon."

"I don't mind."

"You, of course, are excused. You've already given generously of your time today."

She started to suggest that she could manage a few more hours if her expertise was needed, but she knew it wasn't wise to spend more time in Ethan's company. Besides, Saturday was usually reserved for laundry, and she'd already spent more than half the day alone with him. Some distance would be best just now.

Ethan seemed all business when he let her out in front

of her room at the inn later, saying that he could manage unloading without assistance and that he wouldn't dream of taking one more moment of her time that day. After thanking her profusely, he drove away. She couldn't help feeling a little let down. What, after all, was laundry compared to gathering greenery with the handsome pastor of the Mountainview Church of the Savior?

As she washed and dried and folded and hung her laundry, she worked very hard not to think about what it felt like to perch on Ethan's shoulder and be so effortlessly lifted upward or to waste time imagining that he had almost kissed her. She resolved firmly not to believe that his winks were flirtatious rather than merely teasing, or that he had picked the gazebo for their luncheon for any reason other than it had provided a simple form of shelter, breezy though it might have been. She would not assume that he was attracted to her or believe that her attraction to him could have the slightest chance of bearing fruit.

She managed not to think of him, or even how the committee was coming along with its work, more than a few dozen times that whole afternoon and evening, so he caught her off guard the following morning when he called her name from the pulpit. The church had been spruced up with a few sprays of now-wilted greenery and candles from last month's early small-town Christmas in honor of Dale Massey, and they'd sung Christmas carols to properly start off the season, but all that would obviously pale in comparison to what the pastor planned for the true Christmas celebration. Ethan named everyone on the decorating committee when he announced a formal Hanging of the Green service the following Wednesday evening. Had he left the matter there, all would have been well, but he went on to thank Robin specifically and profusely for helping to research and design the decorations, as well as gather the greenery.

Sitting in the pew next to Olivia and Jack, Robin blushed bright red. Livvie seemed to find the whole thing as significant as she'd found his choice for a luncheon site, bumping her shoulder against Robin's and grinning conspiratorially. Robin ignored that, and she intended to ignore Ethan by slipping quietly out a side door after church, but Rosemary Middleton snagged her by the wrist the instant the service ended.

"It's about the chrismon symbols," she began urgently. "Something just isn't right."

She hauled Robin back to the room where the decorating committee had been working and indicated a pile of several dozen white homespun objects on one corner of a table.

"They're limp," Rosemary complained. "We can't hang those on a tree or garland."

The other ladies joined them, everyone crowding into the room at once, and all offering suggestions at the same time.

"We should have glued them to cardboard instead of sewing them together."

"They have to be stuffed with horsehair."

"With straw."

"Why not fiberfill?" Robin asked. "It's not authentic, but it's lightweight and as long as the look is right, it should be fine."

"I have some we can use," Mamie said.

"You better clear it with Pastor first," Rosemary put in.

"Yes, you seem to have influence with the pastor," Nadine commented meaningfully.

Because she was a Shaw and family, though she didn't even know it, Robin let that slide.

"I'll take care of it. In fact, I'll take care of stuffing the chrismon symbols."

"You have to sew yarn loops into the opening, too, so they can be hung," Rosemary pointed out.

"I ought to be able to manage that."

"I'll help," Mamie muttered reluctantly.

Pleased with that offer, the ladies quickly swept the floppy white symbols into a large plastic bag, dropped in a skein of white yarn and handed it over. When she got to her car with it, Ethan was standing on the boardwalk, talking to a few stragglers, without an overcoat despite the biting cold wind.

He looked older, more mature and strangely more masculine in his pastoral collar and dark suit. After shaking hands with a pair of older men, he wheeled about and came straight to her, as if he'd known exactly where she was every minute. Taking the bag from her, he put it into the back of her little hybrid while she gratefully slid down into the front seat. Coming forward to speak to her, he rubbed his bare hands against the cold.

"Settled the quandary of the chrismon symbols, did you?"

"If you don't have any objection to my stuffing them with fiberfill."

He waved a hand. "If you're okay with it, I'm okay with it. There are quite a lot of them, though. Are you sure you can get them done by Wednesday on your own? The plan is to let everyone in the congregation hang one, either on the tree or the garlands."

"Mamie will help."

"Bless Mamie. And you."

For a moment longer, he looked down at her over the rim of her car door as if he would say something more, but then he closed the door, stepped back and slid his hands into his pockets. She pulled the keys from her purse, started up the engine and drove away as quickly as she could. The last she saw of him, glancing back via her rearview mirror, he still stood there, his shoulders hunched against the cold.

She would not think that he had a wishful, almost forlorn expression upon his face. She would not wonder if he had been about to invite her to lunch. She would not believe that he had been waiting for her near her car. She would not, oh, she would *not,* daydream about him just because he was so kind and lighthearted and caring or because he looked so handsome in his black suit and white collar or because he delivered his sermons in such a poignant, down-to-earth fashion and turned his warm brown eyes on her as he thanked her from the pulpit.

Positively, definitely, she would not even contemplate letting anything beyond simple, polite friendship develop between them, for chances were that after Christmas, maybe after the first of the year, she would be leaving Jasper Gulch, one way or another. Either she would tell the Shaws the truth about Lucy and herself and they almost assuredly would reject her, or she would simply slip away without opening that can of worms at all. If the Shaws didn't believe her, the mayor wasn't likely to let her hang around town. He certainly wouldn't let her keep her job, and even if she could find another one, she probably wouldn't be very popular around town. On the other hand, she couldn't see herself keeping quiet and staying here just to live a lie of silence. No, she couldn't plan on staying here in Jasper Gulch.

The very thought brought tears to her eyes, though she didn't know how this quaint little town with its dusty streets, dilapidated bridge and decades-old secrets had managed to work its way into her heart. Even if the Shaws rejected her or never knew she was their kin, she was going to miss Jasper Gulch and the friends she'd made here.

She was very much afraid that she was going to miss Ethan Johnson most of all, and that shouldn't be. That just shouldn't be. Why, she hardly knew the man.

But no matter how often she told herself that, she knew in her heart of hearts that when she left here, she would be taking along a huge load of regret. For the rest of her life, she was going to think of the hunky pastor of the Mountainview Church of the Savior and wonder and wish... and very likely grieve what shouldn't, couldn't, be and never was.

Chapter Five

Somehow when the knock came at her door on Tuesday evening, Robin knew it was Ethan. She looked at Mamie and tried not to blush with excitement. The older woman knotted the thread with which she was attaching a yarn loop to a closed and stuffed fabric chrismon symbol. She trimmed off the thread and tossed the finished decoration aside.

"Wonder who that could be," she said, her plump lips struggling to contain a smile, her needle firmly grasped between thumb and forefinger.

Robin rolled her eyes and went to let him in. He huffed and stamped his dry feet on the bristled mat, spreading a grin around the small, warm room and taking in the mounds of plump chrismon symbols on the table and bed. "Hello."

Mamie nodded, plying her needle on yet another bit of fabric. "Pastor."

"Ethan. Can I get you some coffee or hot apple cider?"

"The cider sounds good, if it's no trouble," he replied to Robin.

"Not if you don't mind the powdered version."

"It's what I use."

"Coming right up, then. Leave your coat on the bed there."

He divested himself of his outerwear and dropped it on the bed before pulling the small armchair closer to the table.

"I've come to help." He carefully added, "And beg another favor."

Robin froze in the act of tearing open the package of cider powder and looked over her shoulder. He had placed a dark purple folder on the edge of the table.

"What sort of favor?"

"I need another reader for the Christmas pageant." At her frown, he hurried on. "There aren't any lines to memorize. You just have to read." He laid his hand on the folder. "It's all right here. Will you look it over, at least? I've marked the part I want you to take."

She might have argued, but Mamie seemed about to burst into laughter, so Robin focused on dumping the powder into the mug, adding water, stirring it together and getting the concoction into the microwave without slamming the door on the small appliance. Once she had the drink heating, she addressed the issue with, she thought, admirable calm. Didn't the man realize how often he left the two of them open to rabid speculation?

"I'll look at it and let you know."

Ethan smiled and rubbed his hands together, asking, "Now, how can I help? I'm afraid I'm no good with needle and thread."

"You stuff, then, and we'll both sew," Mamie ordered, explaining how to poke the airy, weblike fiberfill through the tiny opening at the top of each piece until it was stiff enough to hold its shape. The job was so easy that they already had a large pile awaiting the addition of a small loop of yarn and a few stitches to close the hole and hold everything together. The work truly would go much more quickly with both Mamie and Robin sewing.

Robin picked up the needle and thread she'd set aside earlier and went to work. Ethan chatted as he poked airy bits of polyester into small fabric chrismon symbols, telling them which children were playing which parts in the pageant. When he got to Mary, Mamie gaped.

"Lilibeth Shoemaker? You've got to be kidding."

"I am not," Ethan said quietly but in a tone that brooked no interference. "The committee cleared Lilibeth of any involvement in the disappearance of the time capsule."

"But the note hinted that someone with the initials L.S. was mixed up with the time capsule," Mamie argued. "Who else could it be but Lilibeth Shoemaker?"

"Lucy Shaw," Robin blurted.

After a stunned moment of silence, Ethan shook a wisp of fiberfill at her. "Now, that makes perfect sense. More sense, anyway, than Lilibeth managing to dig up the time capsule, hide it from everybody for some unimaginable purpose, only to hang around here to be accused of the crime, then have it turn up again. Besides, the notes never said L.S. stole anything."

"Well, when you put it like that," Mamie muttered thoughtfully.

"How else can you put it?" Ethan demanded, shaking his head. "No, it's much easier to think that this all has something to do with Lucy's incident at the bridge than a pouty teenager."

Robin's blood ran cold. The *incident,* not the *accident.* Did Ethan know about Lucy's deception? Had he learned that she'd faked her death so she could run off and marry Cyrus?

No, the idea was ludicrous. How could Ethan know that? No one knew but her and the Frazier family, and they certainly wouldn't have told anyone. Would they? Not even to scuttle a relationship between her and the Shaws?

No, they wouldn't stoop that low. Still, someone had written those notes.

For a moment, Robin couldn't catch her breath. Was her family so anxious to ruin her chances to fit in with the Shaws that they would try to sabotage her with anonymous notes? She couldn't bear to think it.

Ethan said something about letting he who was without sin cast the first stone, and Mamie reluctantly admitted that Lilibeth would make as good a Mary as anyone, and the matter smoothed over. Indeed, Robin had already forgotten it and everything else except the possibility that the Frazier/Templetons might be responsible for those notes, which she now felt sure referenced her late great-grandmother. She was so troubled by the possibility that she could only stare blankly at Ethan when, as he was taking his leave a couple hours later, he asked if she would have an answer for him after the service the next evening.

"About the reading. Practice starts Thursday."

"You might as well say yes," Mamie put in, tidying up the table now that the chrismon symbols had all been finished.

"I'm going to need your input anyway," Ethan told Robin apologetically. "On the costumes, the set, the staging, everything."

She sighed, torn. "Fine. If I'm going to be there anyway, I might as well read the part."

"My thoughts exactly," Ethan said happily. "Oh, and one more thing." He leaned close and whispered in her ear, "The bell ropes have arrived." He pulled back, adding, "You haven't forgotten, have you?"

"No, no, I haven't forgotten."

"Great. We'll talk about that later, then. In private."

She nodded and let him out the door. Barely had she closed it again when Mamie crowed, "In private, no less."

Robin gusted out a great sigh. "It's not what you think."

"What I think," Mamie teased saucily, "is that our pastor is finally about to stake a claim."

Robin shook her head. "No. No, it's not like that at all. It has entirely to do with a surprise for the Christmas celebration."

"Uh-huh," Mamie replied doubtfully. "We'll just see about that."

"You will," Robin told her, and suddenly she very much feared that she had spoken the gospel truth. She and Ethan had nothing between them but a centennial-style Christmas celebration, and that was all they ever would, could, have.

The Hanging of the Green service went beautifully, better than even Ethan had envisaged. A group of stalwart men hung the long evergreen garlands, interwoven with strands of electric candles, glass ornaments and sprigs of ivy and holly, beneath the windows at the sides of the church, while Ethan explained the meanings of the various materials used.

The women of the decorating committee came forward to tie on big red bows. Various elders festooned the altar and lectern with swags of greenery, which the ladies also decorated. A beautifully carved crèche was placed upon the altar next to a large Bible open to the Christmas passage in Luke, the whole array set against a backdrop of tapered candles in bronze holders. The tree had been put up in the vestibule and decorated with electric candles and bows. The chrismon symbols were passed out. The children went out to further decorate the tree while the adults finished up inside the sanctuary.

Finally, small candles with paper collars were passed

out and lit. The congregation sang a last carol. Ethan prayed a closing prayer. They blew out the candles and trooped back to the fellowship area for cookies, Christmas punch and mincemeat pie, which tasted surprisingly good. Ethan managed to snag a chair next to Robin. In fact, that chair seemed to have been saved for him, if not by her then by the matchmaking element of his congregation.

Balancing a tiny saucer and cup on one knee, he went straight to the heart of the matter. "Went well, didn't it?"

"It certainly did. I even heard the mayor say so, and Faith is so pleased with the decorations that they're only planning pew bows and some additional candles for her wedding ceremony."

"That's good. I think it looks beautiful myself, even better than I'd hoped."

"It really is lovely," Robin agreed.

"Couldn't have done it without you."

"Oh, you don't have to say that."

"No, I mean it. You're an integral part of the whole scheme. So about tomorrow evening…"

She laughed and wagged a finger at him. "I'm onto you, Pastor Ethan Johnson. Butter up the volunteer and hit her again."

He grinned unrepentantly. "Absolutely. Can you come around seven?"

"I can."

He broke off a bit of cookie and said, "Tell you what, I'll feed you dinner first. To thank you for all you've done."

If it had been anyone else, he'd have assumed she hadn't heard him, for the seconds drew out longer and longer. "Why not?"

He let out a breath he hadn't known he'd been holding. "Fine. What time do you get off work?"

"About five-thirty."

"I'll be at the inn by a quarter of six to pick you up."

"Okay."

"See you then," he said, getting to his feet.

As he walked away, he congratulated himself on his cleverness. It wasn't a date; he did not date. Ever. But no one other than he and Robin would actually know that their being out together was just him repaying a favor. Let the rest of the town assume what they would. He'd gain a bit of breathing space, and Robin would get a decent meal, something he wasn't sure she managed too often, living in that room with its tiny kitchenette at Mamie's. That was what he called a win-win situation.

If he looked forward to it more than he should, well, that was between him and God and a matter for prayer.

"It's not a date," Robin said to Olivia for perhaps the tenth time.

"Half the church heard him ask you out to dinner," Livvie said pointedly. It had been the main topic of conversation for the whole livelong day, much to Robin's exasperation.

"What do I have to do to make you understand?" Robin demanded, shaking her hands in exasperation. "The decorations were only a small part of the plans. There is the pageant on Christmas Eve *and* the Christmas-morning service. We have a lot to discuss, a lot to do. Some of it, I'm not even at liberty to share because Ethan wants it to be a surprise. It's already the eleventh of December. We don't have much time to pull this off."

"And that's why he asked you out to dinner."

"Exactly."

"R*iiii*ght."

Robin threw up her hands. "I give up."

Olivia chuckled. "Good. No reason to fight it."

"Okay," Robin retorted, "it's a date. Can we drop it now?"

"Sure," Olivia returned good-naturedly. "So what are you going to wear?"

"Aaarrggh!" Robin put her hands to her head and doubled over, moaning, "What's wrong with what I'm wearing now?"

"Nothing. For a cactus. In Alaska."

Robin looked up sharply. "Ouch."

"I mean, it's cute enough. If you want to look untouchable."

Robin dropped her shoulders, looking down at the fuzzy green sweater. "Do you give out bandages with your compliments?"

Livvie chuckled. "Look, you're a doll, but you don't do much to play up that fact."

"Why should I?"

Olivia ignored that, remarking, "You could wear that royal blue dress, the one with the elbow-length sleeves and the dip in the back."

"But the matching shoes are open toed."

"So wear your boots with it, the ones with the high heels. And that pretty scarf, knotted in front. And put up your hair."

The very idea was silly, especially if this wasn't an actual date, and yet what could it hurt to look her best? "I'd have to leave early."

"So leave early," Olivia said with a wave of her hand.

"It wouldn't be fair," Robin muttered, but Olivia sent her a droll look.

"I'm the boss. I get to say what's fair."

Robin turned away with a shrug and a nod. Mercifully, nothing more was said on the subject, but when Robin picked up her handbag a few minutes before five, Olivia smiled and remarked that she'd see her tomorrow.

By a quarter to six, Robin stood staring at herself in the mirror. The royal blue dress hugged her slight curves from an inch or two above her knees to her shoulders, where the neckline cut straight across her throat only to dip into a rounded V in the back between her shoulder blades. She'd wound the long, narrow, colorful scarf around her throat, knotted it and allowed the twin black-fringed tails to hang down the front. Olivia had been right to recommend it; the overall effect was to make her neck look long and swan-like, an illusion aided by the simple twisted bun atop her head, while adding color to the monochrome dress. The black boots saved the dress from looking too formal, even added a bit of trendiness and at the same time looked quite feminine and weather appropriate. Still, Robin couldn't help feeling nervous. What if she and Olivia had misread this dinner thing entirely?

Before she could further second-guess, a knock came at her door. Taking a deep breath, she went to throw it open. Ethan stood there, smiling.

"Hey. I hope you're— Wow."

She gulped, wilting. "Too much?"

"Only if there's such a thing as too much spectacular." He stepped inside, took her by the hand and turned her so he could get the full effect. "I mean, *wow*. Great Gulch Grub doesn't deserve…this."

She laughed, feeling very appreciated and admired. "Let me get my things and we'll go."

"Okay." He held the door closed without pushing it all the way into the casing while she picked up her coat and gathered her handbag. Stepping forward, he took her coat from her and helped her shrug into it, his fingertips brushing over her back as the coat slid up into place. "You shouldn't upstage your pastor, you know," he said softly into her ear, his tone teasing.

"Technically," she said wryly, "you're *not* my pastor."

"True," he agreed, stepping up to offer his arm.

She regarded him frankly, aware of the heat in his open

brown gaze. "Does your congregation know what a tease you are?"

"Oh, no," he said, walking her out the door and pulling it closed behind them. "And I'd like to keep it that way."

She laughed and let him escort her to his vehicle. She still didn't know if this was a date or not. At the moment, it didn't seem to matter. She relaxed and allowed herself to enjoy the easy, chatty dinner at the small diner and the somewhat chaotic rehearsal that followed.

As it was the first rehearsal of the pageant, parts were assigned. And then reassigned. And then they were reassigned yet again until everyone was at least nominally happy. Robin remained one of the narrators, along with Ethan himself and Chauncey Hardman, the local librarian.

Single and in her late fifties, Chauncey had at first intimidated Robin with her firm, no-nonsense manner. Robin had been scolded roundly more than once for making noise in the library when she had been the only patron present. But she liked to think that she and the gruff librarian had found a bit of a common bond in their love of history.

Ethan placed the three of them on stools to one side, with Chauncey in the middle.

As they, at long last, took their places, Chauncey cast an appraising glance in Robin's direction and noted, "Your back is awfully bare."

"Not hardly," Ethan said, leaning forward to catch Robin's eye.

Robin frowned.

Chauncey split a look between them, her lips quirking against a smile, and opined, "Well, I suppose you could do worse than a minister. At least he's not a cowboy."

Robin's eyes popped wide, while Ethan, meanwhile, seemed to be either choking or coughing or both behind his fist. Rusty Zidek piped up just then to say he'd changed his mind. He'd rather be a shepherd than a wise man after all. Given his age, an extremely spry ninety-six, Ethan humored him with good-natured patience, engineering a switch with Ellis Cooper, Jasper Gulch's perennial mayoral candidate who always lost to Jackson Shaw. Though at least twenty-five years younger than Jackson, Ellis had some definite ideas about what was and was not good for the community, and many agreed with him.

In addition to the usual players, they were to have a virtual legion of cherubic angels and a whole herd of woolly sheep capable of walking the aisle on two feet before dropping to all fours at the front. Olivia's father-in-law, Mick McGuire, had agreed to serve as wrangler for the real animals. His young stepchildren were going to be in the pageant anyway, he reasoned, so he might as well take part. Jack and the two unmarried Shaw brothers, Austin and Adam, had volunteered to put the set together. The major actors were teenagers, with a sprinkling of adults and numerous children, who required numerous adult overseers, mostly women.

"And I need your input on nearly all of it," he explained afterward, taking Robin aside. "For instance, the printed programs. What do you think of putting that old photo on the front?"

"Oh, that's brilliant," she declared. "That way everyone will see at once what we're trying to do."

"My thoughts exactly. I'm just not sure how to put it together."

"Leave that to me," Robin suggested. "I have an idea."

"Bless you!" Ethan intoned, giving her a quick hug. "I knew I'd found a treasure in you."

A treasure? Glancing around, Robin spied several knowing smirks. That one word would be enough to keep the town gossips going for weeks.

What really surprised Robin, though, was the way Rusty Zidek watched them with such obvious interest, his craggy, lined face both avid and pensive. It wasn't the first time she'd caught Rusty staring at her these past months. She'd thought at first that she was imagining the way his gaze seemed to follow her every movement, but he really didn't even try to hide it. Lately, his stare seemed so knowing that it unnerved her.

Though aged, whipcord lean and jerky tough, with slightly stooped shoulders and thick silver hair, including an audacious mustache, Rusty gave the impression of permanence and strength. A widower, he refused to sit on the sidelines and decay. Instead, he rattled around town in his ancient Jeep or, weather permitting, on an ATV, took part in all the centennial celebrations and generally seemed to live life to the fullest. Robin couldn't help admiring the old fellow; she just wondered what he found so interesting about her in particular.

Questions about costuming eventually distracted her from thoughts of Rusty and everything else. Thankfully, Rosemary Middleton, Mamie Fidler and Allison Douglas had agreed to take on the shopping, fitting and sewing, but they wanted Robin's okay on everything.

When the recorded bells played their usual toll at the nine o'clock hour, things started to wind down, but the time approached 10:00 p.m. before Robin found herself alone with Ethan in the evergreen-redolent sanctuary. Looking a little shell-shocked, he turned to her and asked, "Have I lost my mind?"

She smiled. "We'll see."

"It seemed like a good idea at the time," he told her with a sheepish grin.

"I think it's going to turn out well—as well, hopefully, as the decorations."

"God willing."

They started walking toward the back of the sanctuary, and once there, he began turning off lights.

"I'll tell you one thing. This is certainly an evening I won't forget," he said around a grin, closing the sanctuary door and waiting for her to cross the vestibule before he joined her, "if only because of that dress."

She twisted to glance over her shoulder. "Is it terribly immodest, then?"

"Not at all," he assured her. "You just wear it so very well."

She blushed with pleasure. "Thank you. It's just the way Miss Hardman remarked about it, I wasn't sure."

"Miss Hardman is not the final arbiter of taste around here, not of my taste anyway." Robin smiled, and he took her coat from the closet there to help her into it. "Rusty sure couldn't take his eyes off you."

"I noticed that. What was that about do you suppose?"

"The man obviously liked what he saw," Ethan said, shrugging into his own coat.

"Oh, he's old enough to be my grandfather. My great-grandfather, actually."

"Doesn't mean he can't appreciate a beautiful woman."

"Ethan Johnson, you *are* a flirt," she scolded lightly, smiling broadly.

Laughing, they buttoned up, shut off the last of the lights and stepped out into the cold, still night. Ethan locked the door, took her elbow and walked her to the car, where he handed her down into the passenger seat. Back at the inn, he insisted on walking her to her room and waiting until she'd flipped on the interior light, but he didn't come in.

"Thanks for all your help," he said, shuffling his feet.

She chuckled. "You're welcome. Thank you for dinner. You know, I wasn't really sure if this was a date or not."

Bowing his head, he shrugged and suddenly admitted, "To tell you the truth, it wasn't meant to be, but somehow..." He curled a finger beneath her chin, tilted her face up, dipped his head and brushed his lips across hers. "Good night, Robin."

"Good night, Ethan," she murmured, stunned.

He slipped off into the night, leaving her as confused as she was delighted.

Chapter Six

When Robin called the next day to say that she'd like Ethan to approve a design for the Christmas Eve program, he couldn't have been more relieved. He'd greatly feared that he'd overstepped badly with that kiss the night before, and he wasn't sure how to approach her when next they met. They weren't due for another practice until the following Wednesday, and he hated to let the matter simmer until then, so he was all too happy to spend his Friday afternoon at the museum looking at graphic designs on the computer. Hopefully, he would find an opportunity to apologize for that kiss and set things right between them. The last thing he wanted to do was mislead Robin.

"I like the one with the photo tilted," he decided after viewing several options, "but maybe we could frame it with greenery to give it some color."

"Or," she said, beginning to click her mouse, "we could do this."

She quickly layered in an arrangement of lit Advent candles grounded in holly. She overlaid that with the old tintype photo, tilted at the angle he liked and typed in the necessary titling with a red font, picking up the color of the berries in the holly.

"Perfect," he declared.

"We can do the printing here if you like," she volunteered. "I've already spoken to Olivia about it. But the church will have to provide the paper."

"I'll pick up the paper tomorrow morning," he said. "I'll even buy the ink if you'll tell me what to get."

She wrote down the details for him, and they agreed that he would hand off the paper and ink the following evening when she stopped by the church to look at the fabric and patterns for the pageant costumes. The ladies were shopping today and taking measurements tomorrow but were reluctant to cut the fabric without her approval.

"I'm sure it'll be fine, but they insist," she told him.

"Sounds like they're becoming as dependent on you as I am," he said, smiling at her.

"I don't know about that," she muttered, looking away.

He steeled himself and said the words he'd prayed over and rehearsed. "Robin, I want to apologize about that kiss and also—"

"I wish you wouldn't," she interrupted, keeping her gaze averted. "I feel foolish enough as it is."

Shocked, he felt his eyebrows leap upward. "What have you got to feel foolish about?"

"I—I thought it was a date. Well, *I* didn't really, but Olivia and the others…"

"I let them think that," he admitted apologetically. "I wanted them to think it, honestly. It's just… All the matchmaking, it gets so tiresome, and I thought, since they're going to assume *anyway* that any young, single woman I spend time with is of special interest to me, well, then, why not let them?"

"I understand," she told him quickly. "It's okay."

"I'm so glad!" he exclaimed, terribly relieved.

"But they'll realize their mistake soon enough," she went on briskly. "Before long they'll see that I'm not the sort of woman for a man like you."

"Now, why would you say that?" he asked, puzzled.

She shook her head, replying only, "You need a better woman than me."

Stunned, he muttered, "You have that backward."

He'd always thought that she was pleasingly humble for so accomplished a young woman, just the sort to make a good wife for a clergyman, any clergyman but him. This, though, was crazy. She was too good for a man who had hung out with murderers, a man with a family member behind bars and another who couldn't bring herself even to speak to him.

Gulping, Ethan sent up a silent prayer.

You changed me, Lord, and set my feet on an entirely different path. I promised You that I wouldn't ask for more, not for myself. For Robin, though, I ask Your greatest blessings.

He couldn't believe that there were better women than Robin Frazier in this world. Certainly none deserved love more than she did.

The Christmas story was one of unbridled, unsurpassed love, the willingness of God to be born as a perfect baby into an imperfect world, to live a perfect life and then lay it down again for that same imperfect world in order to bridge the gulf between humanity and Himself. Christmas, Ethan was reminded, was a season of wonders, as God was the God of wonders.

As Ethan watched Robin manipulate the image on the computer screen, the fifth verse of Psalm 40 ran through Ethan's mind.

Many, Lord my God, are the wonders You have done, the things You planned for us. None can compare with You; were I to speak and tell of Your deeds, they would be too many to declare.

Surely it wouldn't be too much for such a God to bless this generous young woman who so willingly helped, so quickly forgave and so humbly discounted her own worth. Such a woman would be all too easy to love.

The sun put in its first appearance at 7:58 in the morning on Saturday the thirteenth of December. Robin knew this because the radio in her car announced the time as she pulled to a stop in front of the church, two minutes early for her appointment with the costume committee. The sun had just forced its blazing rays over the horizon, lining the mountains to the east with a streak of molten gold that bounced off the glass of her rearview mirror and dazzled her for a second, so that she had to close her eyes until they adjusted to the spreading glory. Still half-blinded, she got out of the car and started toward the boardwalk to the education wing. A hand clasped onto her wrist, arresting her progress. Thinking it one of the women, for Ethan's hand had a stronger, less ropy, leathery feel about it, she smiled and shielded her eyes with her hand. The wrinkled, mustachioed visage of Rusty Zidek came into view, shadowed beneath the deep, curled brim of a dirty brown felt cowboy hat.

"You're Lucy's gal, aren't you?"

The shock of hearing her late great-grandmother's real name sent Robin mentally reeling. "What? I don't… What are you saying?"

"You got her look about you. Well, more her ma's look, I s'pose. You're a dead ringer for Elaine Shaw."

Robin felt her jaw drop. "How did you…?"

"Aw, don't worry. Won't no one else see it because they didn't know Ezra and Elaine, but I did. With the right clothes and hairstyle, you could just about pass as old Missus Shaw's twin, at least when she was young. I know 'cause I saw pictures."

He was wrong about one thing: someone else *had* noticed. Some time ago while looking through some old photos, Cord Shaw had noted the similarity between Robin and Ezra Shaw's bride. Robin had laughed it off, but that photo had proved to her as nothing else could have the veracity of her great-grandmother's story. Robin swallowed and forced a smile.

"That's very interesting, but I have a meeting to attend, so if you'll pardon me..."

She pulled free and took a step away, but he halted her with a simple statement. "I know Lucy didn't die when that car went off the bridge."

Gasping, Robin whirled to face him. "What did you say?"

He pushed back his hat and hung his thumbs in the belt loops of his jeans. "I was there. I was just a boy, but I followed Lucy that night. I saw how she and Cyrus ran that Model T off the bridge and slipped away together, and I kept their secret all these years 'cause that's what Lucy asked me to do. Her pa didn't have any right to force her to marry against her heart, even to save the bank."

"You know about that, too?"

"I heard the talk. They said there was something fishy going on at the bank, that Silas Massey left town a rich man in 1924, though everyone knew he'd made some bad investments. Ezra Shaw denied the bank was low on cash, but some folks withdrew their money anyhow. They said he used his own fortune to cover the loss. In '26, that feller Victor Fitzhugh offered to buy into the bank, give it a big infusion of cash, *if* Lucy would marry him."

"How do you know this?" Robin demanded.

"Lucy told me herself. Said she'd rather die than marry old Fitzhugh."

Those had been Lucy's last words to her father, in fact, and she had regretted them, but not running away to marry the love of her life, or so she'd told Robin.

"Can't blame her," Rusty said. "Fitzhugh was nearly

her daddy's age, a big, hard man, all jowls and whiskers, and her just sixteen years old. 'Sides, she was in love with Cyrus, and he was in love with her. That's why nobody questioned it when he went away after the accident."

"What happened after Cyrus went away?" Robin asked.

"Fitzhugh took his money and went back where he came from," Rusty explained. "Old Ezra hung on at the bank, even in '29 when the big crash came, but by '32 he had to give up. Back then the Shaws were land poor like all the rest of the ranchers, but they held on. Gotta respect them for that, especially as they knew about the gold in the time capsule and didn't touch it. They stayed true to the agreement about that."

"Gold!" Robin erupted.

"And lots of it," Rusty told her. "Lucy said that one day the Shaws and Masseys would all inherit a fortune when the time treasure was dug up. She said Silas wanted to go back on the agreement and dig it up when his investments went bust, but Ezra wouldn't allow it, and that's why Silas looted the bank. He said he was taking the Massey share whether the Shaws approved or not."

"So that's why the time capsule was stolen," Robin mused. "Gold."

"That's my theory," Rusty acknowledged. "So I got to thinking." He tapped his temple with a gnarled finger. "Who'd know about that treasure? And it couldn't be anybody but the Shaws, more like *a* Shaw, and my money's on the mayor himself."

"Surely not!" Robin insisted more loudly than she'd intended. "Everyone says Pete Daniels is the culprit. Why else would he leave town like that?"

Rusty grimaced. "Think about it. How would Daniels know about the gold? If the gold is in the time capsule when it's opened, what's the mayor's excuse for keeping the bridge closed? He can't say there's no money to pay for it anymore."

"But Dale Massey is underwriting the reopening of the bridge."

Rusty nodded, cackling gleefully. "And don't you know that sticks in Jackson Shaw's craw! All the more reason to cut the Masseys out of the inheritance. Lucy told me that the Massey and the Shaw heirs were to share it equally."

Robin blinked. If what Rusty said was true—and she had no reason to doubt him—then the fact that she had kept quiet all these months about her connection to Lillian/ Lucy and the Shaws had just become exponentially more complicated. If she spoke up now, Jackson might think she was after the gold!

But where did Pete Daniels fit into all this? Why flee town if he was innocent of any crime?

She narrowed her eyes at Rusty Zidek, demanding, "Why are you telling me what you know? And why are you telling it now after all these years?"

"'Cause," he said, "Lucy'd want you to have your share of that gold."

"I'm not here for gold!" Robin snapped, though everyone would think so if she told them the truth about herself and her great-grandmother now.

Rusty's weathered face folded into a series of deep crevices. "Well, now, that's fine. You know what the Good Book says, the love of money is the root of all kinds of evil. But I can't look into your eyes without seeing my sweet Lucy's, and I know she'd want you to have everything coming to you, money, family, all of it. And I've been trying to help you get it."

Understanding dawned. "You've been leaving those notes around town!"

One note, back in August, had told the committee looking into the disappearance of the time capsule to "think about L.S." Another note had shown up in November after the time capsule had reappeared. That note had warned that something important was missing from the container and been signed with the cryptic cypher "LS4EVER." People around town had assigned the initials to Lilibeth Shoemaker, but the teenager had disavowed any connection to the disappearance of the time capsule and whatever it had contained, and nearly everyone had believed her. The committee had cleared her of involvement.

Rusty nodded. "I'd do it again, too. Now *you* gotta do what *you* gotta do."

"What's that supposed to mean?"

"You gotta confront the mayor about this."

"Me? Why me?"

"You're Lucy's granddaughter."

"Great-granddaughter," Robin corrected, wincing when she realized that she'd just confirmed his suspicions.

He showed her a wide smile beneath that prodigious mustache, featuring a bright gold tooth in front. "Yep. That's what I figured." His filmy old eyes blurred, and his chin wobbled. "Lucy and Cyrus did good for themselves. Now, you do her proud, you hear?" With that, he turned and shambled away.

Dismayed, Robin headed in the opposite direction. Didn't he realize that what he asked of her was impossible, now more so than ever? It was one thing to impose herself on the preeminent family in the area as a long-lost relative and another to do so after keeping her silence on the matter for nearly six months now, but to reveal herself as a member of the family after learning a fabulous inheritance might be claimed was unthinkable. They would surely brand her a gold digger! Literally.

Oh, how had she gotten herself into this mess? The more she dwelled on it throughout the morning, while approving fabrics and patterns for the pageant costumes, the more convinced she became that the Shaws would revile and reject her if she came forward now.

She toyed with the idea of going to Ethan and laying out the whole problem, seeking his advice, but the thought of confessing her lies to him made her want to weep. He had kissed her. Very innocently, perhaps, and he obviously regretted it. Nothing could ever come of it. Nevertheless, he had kissed her, and she'd dreamed about that kiss, no doubt making much more of it than she should.

They had worked together for weeks now, and all the while she had kept her true identity and purpose from him. How could she tell him the truth and ever face him again afterward? She could almost see his disappointment and feel the change in him. The very idea made her heart hurt; so did the notion of never seeing Ethan again, but how could she stay in Jasper Gulch with this secret hanging over her head, especially since Rusty Zidek had confirmed his suspicions about her?

If she didn't confront the mayor as Rusty wanted, would Rusty divulge her true identity? She couldn't trust that he wouldn't, perhaps not right away but eventually. If he spoke up, she'd either have to deny his claims—in other words, lie—or try to prove them, but all she had as proof were her great-grandmother's words, a name and an old photograph.

Robin didn't know what to do. She couldn't go to the Shaws with the flimsy proof she had, she couldn't count on Rusty to keep quiet indefinitely and she couldn't confess to Ethan. She finally came to the conclusion that she would have to leave Jasper Gulch, but she couldn't go while Ethan was so dependent on her. In the end, she decided that she would stay until after Christmas. It was only twelve days away. She would help Ethan provide his congregation with the centennial Christmas celebration that he envisioned. If God allowed and Rusty was kind, she might even hang around for the dedication and opening of the museum on New Year's Eve, but then she would leave Jasper Gulch and the friends she'd made here. And, sadly, any hope of connecting with her Shaw family.

She would leave behind any chance of fulfilling her great-grandmother's deathbed wish for her, any chance of being accepted by her Montana family.

And Ethan.

She would leave Ethan and even the dream of anything they might have had together.

In fact, it was probably best just to nip that in the bud now before she managed to break her own heart. If it wasn't already too late.

Christmas carols had never sounded so merry to Ethan as they did that Sunday morning. He and Robin had toiled side by side the day before, though each had been absorbed with separate responsibilities. Nevertheless, he had been keenly aware of her every moment of every hour. She had seemed distracted, even flustered, at times, and he'd been almost too busy himself to do more than give her a passing suggestion here or there. Every time, she'd regained her equilibrium and forged on with the work at hand. He'd found himself taking great pride in her.

Without even realizing it or him intending it, she'd stepped into the role of helpmeet, acting as his partner in many ways. The idea both disturbed and entranced him, so much so that for the first time he began to question his conviction that God meant him to remain alone.

She'd looked exhausted at the end of the day, tempting him to ask her to join him for dinner. He'd refrained, fearing his own motives. Instead, he planned ahead and laid up a Sunday meal, a hearty soup, made mostly from a mix, that bubbled away in a Crock-Pot in the church kitchen as he preached.

Who, after all, could mistake a bowl of soup in the church kitchen for a date? They'd go over the checklist for the pageant and the Christmas service to see what remained to be done, enjoy a hot meal and perhaps find a moment of privacy in which to discuss roping the bells. He could almost smell the soup from the pulpit and eagerly looked forward to that moment when he could take her hand in his as they bowed their heads in a prayer of thanks over the simple meal.

After the service, he dutifully stood at the back of the sanctuary, offering his hand to everyone who came to him. Robin trudged up the center aisle, her handbag hanging from her shoulder by a long strap. He offered her a smile, along with his hand, and pulled her to his side.

"Could you wait with me a minute? I have something to ask you. Just let me finish up here first."

She seemed a tad reluctant, and who could blame her? He'd heaped mountains of responsibility on her slender shoulders of late.

"Nothing to make more work for you," he promised, ducking his head.

She smiled wanly and stayed put, shifting her weight from foot to dainty foot. Finally, they were alone in the sanctuary, sunshine gilding its windows and igniting a golden glow in the pale woodwork dressed with fragrant evergreens and cheerful holly, the big red bows and white chrismon symbols lending a true holiday feel to the place. Anticipation welled up in Ethan.

"Will you take Sunday dinner with me? I have it pretty much ready in the church kitchen. I thought we could go over a few things in peace and quiet, away from the chaos."

Her face fell before he got all the words out. "Oh, Ethan, I don't know. I, um, I'm so tired. I—I think I must be coming down with something." She lifted a hand to her throat. He noticed that her fingers shook. Automatically, he reached up to feel her forehead, but she darted back a step. "I—I probably should've stayed away this morning. Don't want to expose anyone to…anything."

"I've made soup," he said, gesturing helplessly. "At least take some with you."

She shook her head. "No. No, I couldn't. I…I couldn't eat now. I just couldn't." With that she turned and hurried out into the vestibule.

He went after her. "Maybe I ought to drive you home."

"No, please. I just…" She reached into the coat closet, grabbed her overcoat and ran from the building without even bundling up first.

Concerned, Ethan followed her out onto the boardwalk and watched as she hurried to her car while frantically digging in her bag for her keys. She dumped her things into the vehicle then climbed in after them and was driving away in mere seconds.

A shiver of foreboding went through him. She didn't seem desperately ill, merely *desperate*. Now that he really thought about it, she'd acted a little distant and uncomfortable yesterday. He'd thought it a matter of her taking on such a prominent role in the holiday preparations, but could it be that their nondate had affected her more than he'd realized?

Had he hurt her with that impulsive kiss and his apology afterward? It had hardly been a kiss at all, really, but had it been a step too far for Robin? She was certainly avoiding him. Could it because of the apology?

Was it possible that Robin actually *liked* him? She'd said that he needed a better woman than her, but he'd thought that was her humility talking. Could she think that *he* judged her as lacking, that *he* didn't think she was good enough for him?

The truth was just the opposite! She was everything for which he could possibly hope, everything wonderful he could possibly imagine—and for which he never dared to ask.

He didn't know what to do now. His hand drifted up to the collar at his throat, and he turned back to the church, always the source of his greatest solace. As he walked, he began to murmur a prayer.

"Lord, I'm in a quandary here. I need some guidance."

As he went through the motions of preparing and eating his lonely lunch, he talked it out with God, and in the end he understood that he was as much pastor as man, though with Robin he seemed to have a difficult time remembering that. She might not be a formal member of his congregation, but she had rendered much aid to him and the church. He owed her pastoral care.

He waited until after the evening service, unsurprised that she did not put in an appearance. After everyone had left, he packaged up the remaining soup, some bread, juice and canned fruit cocktail and drove over to the inn. Knocking, he announced himself, then prayed that she would open the door for him. When she finally did, she wore a fluffy pink bathrobe over a pair of old jeans and an oversize T-shirt, her stockinged feet stuffed into a pair of old slippers that had seen better days. With her pale gold hair piled on top of her head in a wobbly bun, she couldn't have looked more adorable, despite her red-rimmed eyes and swollen nose. He couldn't decide if she'd been crying or if she was truly ill. Either way, she needed a bit of comfort from someone. He held out the sack of foodstuffs.

"I thought you might feel more like eating now."

Nodding, she took the brown paper bag from him. "I am kind of hungry. Thank you."

"It's chicken noodle soup," he said, standing in the open doorway as she carried the bag to the tiny kitchenette. "And some other stuff."

"Looks good," she said listlessly, rummaging around in

the bag. She glanced back over her shoulder at him, saying, "You're letting all the warm air out."

He stepped inside and pushed the door almost shut, waiting while she carefully set the food on the narrow counter.

"I'll enjoy this," she said in a nasal tone, her back to him. "Thank you again."

"My pleasure," he told her.

She folded the bag, her slender fingers smoothing each crease precisely, before turning to face him. Then they both spoke at once.

"About this morning…"

"You're more than I deserve."

Stunned into momentary silence, they took each other's measure, both frowning. Then again, they spoke at the same time.

"What about this morning?"

"I don't understand." She waved him into silence. "What do you mean, more than you deserve?

He didn't know what had possessed him to say it, but now he had to explain it. Licking his lips, he picked his words. "Any man would be blessed to have you, Robin, myself included. Never think otherwise."

She turned her back on him, and his heart dropped like a stone. He fought the urge to reach for her, and despite his best intentions found himself standing behind her, his hands on her upper arms. He could feel her trembling, and pitched his voice low to hide his urgency.

"Robin, what is it?"

"Don't ask," she croaked.

Something was very wrong here, much more than he'd assumed. "You can tell me anything."

She slipped out of his reach, folding her arms. "Please don't ask. Please, Ethan."

He understood then that whatever it was, she felt that

she couldn't share it with him. His thoughts circled back to the things that he had not yet shared with her: a girl-friend dead on the streets of Los Angeles because of his choice of friends, a father in prison, a sister who wouldn't even speak to him.

Perhaps her secrets would not carry the same weight as his, or perhaps they would. It really didn't matter. Nothing she could tell him would make him think any less of her. But could he trust that she could truly say the same about him?

"When you're ready to talk," Ethan said softly, "I'm here."

She nodded, but he left there with the impression that she never intended to say a word about what was really bothering her. That being the case, how could he possibly share what was in his own heart? Perhaps, he told himself, that was as it should be. He determined to place the matter at God's feet and leave it there.

On his way home, he determinedly went over his plans for the Christmas celebration and quickly realized that the next thing on his agenda was special music. He'd barely dropped his keys into the dish on the side table in his tiny entry hall when he recalled that he had some old music to go through. He put that at the top of his to-do list for Monday morning.

Then he took off his collar, put on some sweats and went down into his basement to pump iron and talk to God.

Who else, after all, could he trust with his secrets?

Chapter Seven

Feeling guilty, according to Robin's great-grandmother, was a waste of time and a distraction. Guilt, she had maintained, was meant to spur one to repentance. After true repentance, it served no useful purpose. It merely sidetracked one from doing what one ought to do, most specifically, performing God's will. Recalling that sage advice, Robin realized over a bowl of Ethan's soup what she had to do about the lie she'd let him believe.

Though technically she'd felt miserable and hadn't wanted to expose anyone to her lousy mood, she was as guilty of untruth as if she'd claimed outright to have a cold. Once she'd apologized to God, she began to feel a bit better, but the real relief came the next afternoon when Ethan arrived at the museum bearing a box filled with books, photos and papers, including a stack of old music scores.

"I was going through some things," he explained, setting down his burden on Robin's desk, "and I realized that this lot belongs with you now. I'd like copies for the church, but I didn't think I ought to make them myself. I wouldn't want to degrade anything, especially the hand-copied pieces. Some of this sheet music looks to be nearly a hundred and fifty years old."

Astonished, Robin picked up her phone and asked Livvie to come in at her first opportunity, adding, "You won't believe what Ethan's brought in."

Livvie replied that she needed a few minutes. That gave Robin enough time to set things right with Ethan.

"Thank you for bringing this in. Before Livvie gets here, I just want to apologize for yesterday."

"You don't owe me any apologies, Robin."

"I do. I wasn't ill. I was upset."

He showed no surprise. Instead, his warm brown gaze captured and held hers. She could almost feel his tender embrace. "Care to tell me about it?"

"No. I…" She shook her head, casting her gaze downward. "I just can't. Not now."

"All right," he said, his voice like silk. "Whenever you're ready."

She lifted her head in an agony of doubt. "What if I'm never ready?"

The sadness and empathy of his smile made her want to cry. "We all have secrets at some time, Robin. But not from God. He knows all, and He waits to see how well and wisely we handle what we keep from each other. Scripture commands us to walk as children of light. That means that all things that are kept in darkness must eventually come to light. Pray about it, and I trust you'll see your way through."

"But I may have already waited too long. What if it's already too late?"

"It's never too late. God will make a way."

Oh, how she wanted to believe that, but if that was true, then why hadn't Great-Grandma Lillian—or rather, Lucy—come back and told her family what she'd done? Why hadn't she confessed to faking her own death so she could be with Great-Grandpa Cyrus?

Livvie came into the room then with a pair of gloves in hand. Robin took hers from a drawer and pulled them on so they could go through the box without damaging its contents.

"Oh, this is good stuff, Ethan," Livvie said as they spread out the contents on the worktable in Robin's office. "How did you come across it?"

He explained about going through old music files looking for appropriate arrangements for the Christmas services.

"That reminds me, Robin," he said, "we're putting together a women's a cappella group to sing on Christmas morning. I wonder if you might be interested."

She immediately began hedging. "Oh, I don't know if—"

"I get that you're already loaded up with responsibilities," Ethan broke in smoothly, "but you told me that you sung in college, and it's just one song. Plus, you'll be out of sight the whole time." He pulled a folded sheet of music from the chronologically displayed papers on the table and handed it to her.

Cautiously, she opened it and began to read both music and words. It wasn't really a Christmas carol but a song about bright, pure, holy love. The music was written in a simple but haunting four-part harmony that would play to good effect in a cappella. It occurred to her that the addition of a pair of simple handbells could make this a very Christmassy song indeed.

"I don't suppose you have any handbells, do you?"

Ethan's gaze quickened. "As a matter of fact, we do."

"Wouldn't they sound sweet at the beginning and again just here?" She pointed to a rest in the music score. "And here."

He beamed at her. "I'll take that as a yes. And the handbells will be ready for practice on Wednesday after the midweek service. Oh, and don't forget pageant practice tomorrow evening."

"Of course," Robin murmured.

Glancing at Olivia, he added, "I trust you will copy the music for us."

Smiling wryly, Olivia put a hand on her hip. "How many copies?"

"Four should do it. Uh, better make that five. And thank you. I've already blown my events budget, big-time."

"Well, cheer up," Olivia said. "It's almost the end of the year. In two weeks, the new year's budget will kick in."

"I was talking about the new year's budget," he divulged, heading for the door. "This had better be a Christmas to remember," he told them, grinning, "because it's going to have to hold us for a long while." With that, he strode from the room.

Robin looked at Olivia, and they both burst out laughing.

"Guess we'd better do what we can to make this centennial Christmas a success," Robin proclaimed.

"One of us," Livvie said drily, "is already giving it her all. Why don't you just admit you're interviewing for the position of pastor's wife?" Olivia teased. "Seems to me you've practically got the job."

The room darkened, as if suddenly engulfed by a cloud. Robin ducked her head, pretending to focus on the materials spread out across the worktable.

"Don't be ridiculous. I'm not fit to be a pastor's wife."

Pastor's wives did not lie. They did not hang around for months without divulging their true connections to people. They did not withhold vital information, especially from family. They did not disappoint their parents and grandparents and hide things from the men about whom they cared, good men, honest men.

"I don't think the pastor in question agrees with you," Livvie quipped. "And I notice you don't deny that you want the position."

"Will you stop being silly and get to work," Robin snapped.

Obviously stung, Olivia drew back. "Sure," she said after a moment. "Didn't mean to step on your toes."

"It's not that," Robin said, fighting to keep her voice level. "It's just silly, that's all."

"I don't see what's silly about it," Livvie remarked softly. "He obviously likes you a lot, and I thought you liked him, too."

"I do like him," Robin admitted, still not looking at her friend and coworker. "But nothing's going to come of it, Livvie. Nothing can."

"I don't understand. Why not?"

"That's our business," Robin whispered. "Please, just let it be."

Olivia remained silent and still for a moment; then she squeezed Robin's shoulder and briskly said, "Let's get these things cataloged. I'm thinking these old hymnals and this sheet music would make nice additions to that display of guitars and harmonicas."

"These photos of the old pump organ would make nice backdrops, too," Robin said, grateful that the subject of her and Ethan had been dropped.

They chatted about the best process for blowing up and cropping the photographs and how to mount them in the back of the display. Meanwhile, Robin pictured in her mind's eye the poignant smile that Ethan had given her and heard his words whisper in her ears.

We all have secrets, Robin. But not from God.... All things that are kept in darkness must eventually come to light....

If Ethan was right, then eventually, one way or another, her secrets would all be revealed. Either she would tell them or Rusty would. She toyed with the idea of asking Rusty to keep his own counsel on the matter. He had kept

her great-grandmother's secret after all—for decades! It
didn't seem fair to ask him to keep hers on top of that, but
she didn't know what else to do. Then Ethan's final piece
of advice wafted through her memory.

Pray about it....

She could do that, and hope that Ethan's faith in her
was not misplaced.

Pageant practice went smoothly on Tuesday, mostly
because it involved only the older participants: the narrators, Mary, Joseph, the innkeeper, a single angel, the elder
shepherds and the wise men. As a shepherd, Rusty was
there, and Robin made sure to catch him after the practice.

She timed it so that they were outside on the boardwalk
before she caught up to him, but he seemed to be expect-
ing her, turning to study her until she caught up to him.

"Got something to say to me?"

"Let's get out of this cold first," she suggested, aiming
her key fob at her car and unlocking it.

"Don't mind if I do." He hobbled over and opened the
passenger door, while Robin hurried around and let herself in on the driver's side. As they both settled down into
their seats, he said, "You haven't been to see the mayor."

"No, not yet. And I hope you'll keep my true identity
to yourself until I decide exactly what to do and when and
how to do it."

"You mean until you decide whether to tell the Shaws
the truth or not, don't you?"

Robin took a deep breath. "I'm just not sure what purpose it would serve at this point."

"Tell me this. What would Lucy want you to do?"

Sighing, Robin admitted, "She wanted me to tell them."

"That's gotta be the deciding factor for me," he declared, "but I won't get out in front of you on this."

In other words, if she left without telling the Shaws the

full truth, he would inform them of what he'd seen the night the car had gone off the bridge and of Robin's full identity, but not before then.

"I understand," she told him. "Thank you."

"I'm not doing it for you," he said in a gravelly voice. "I'm doing it for Lucy. I was always half-sweet on Lucy. She was special, Lucy was, and I don't aim to fail her."

"My great-grandmother would be very moved to think she inspired such devotion," Robin said quietly.

"You think she doesn't know?" the old man scoffed. "If heaven's anything like I think it is, she knows that and more."

Robin smiled and shifted in her seat. "Can I ask your opinion about something else? I've been thinking about this quite a bit lately, and I'm puzzled. My great-grandmother was a God-fearing lady. She had great faith and believed in doing the right thing, so why did she never come back and let her family know she was alive?"

Rusty lifted his hat and scratched his head. "Well, now, I can't say for sure, but I figure she didn't come back while Ezra was alive 'cause she knew he'd blame Cyrus and probably try to ruin him. Then, too, she gave up her share of the Shaw Ranch and all the Shaw holdings by faking her death. There'd have been legal problems if she'd showed up alive, even after Cyrus had passed. It might even have called into question the legality of her marriage, especially if she wasn't married as herself."

"Oh, I hadn't thought of any of that."

"Kinda like Jacob after he stole Esau's birthright. It was God's will for Jacob to get the blessing, but the way he went about it caused some problems, if you see what I mean?"

"I think I do."

"Of course, Lucy was young when she came up with that plan," Rusty mused.

"She told me that she didn't regret it," Robin divulged, "except that it had cost me the connection with my family."

"You know," Rusty said, "Esau eventually forgave Jacob. Seems to me you oughta offer folks the same chance. Then again," he added sagely, "maybe you're thinking that you don't want to ruin a certain someone's Christmas."

She blushed at that and stammered, "I—I j-just w-want to get through the centennial c-celebrations."

"Mmm," he hummed, opening the car door, "and the pastor just wants your expert opinion on every little thing." Before she could form any sort of rejoinder to that, he crawled up out of the car and closed the door.

Turning up the collar of his coat, he stepped up onto the boardwalk. Then he flipped her a wave and shuffled off toward his old Jeep.

Cold, Robin started the engine of her car. She glanced toward the front of the church as she put the transmission into gear and prepared to back out of the parking space. Ethan stood in the doorway of the vestibule, his hands in his pockets, shoulders hunched against the cold. With a nod of his chin, he turned back into the building. Obviously he'd seen Rusty get out of her car and must have wondered what they'd talked about, and just as obviously, he wasn't going to ask.

She wondered why that made her both grateful and sad.

Keeping his own counsel was a pastor's stock-in-trade, and to Ethan that meant not only keeping quiet about what his congregants told him, except where someone's safety might be in question, but also about what he observed on occasion. Not asking unwanted questions was proving to be more difficult, however, especially in Robin's case.

He couldn't for the life of him imagine what she and Rusty Zidek would sit in the cold to discuss. Still, if Robin remained unwilling to confide in him, Ethan didn't know what he could do about it. Pestering her was not likely to help. Either she trusted him or she didn't. Then again, why should she trust him with her secrets when he hadn't trusted her with his?

He thought about that when he saw her walk down the aisle to take a seat for the midweek service. She had pulled back from him, and no matter how often he told himself that was a good thing, he couldn't quite make himself believe it. The previous pastor's advice had been well meaning and perhaps even correct, but by following it, Ethan had made himself a hypocrite.

Sadly, that realization had come too late. He had planned a series of sermons about all the second chances God had given His people throughout the Bible, and in those sermons Ethan had planned to gradually reveal the details of his past to his congregation. He'd intended to tell them how God had rescued him from the path of destruction and set him on the path to wholeness, but he feared what such revelations would do now. How could he expect Robin to confide in him when he kept his own secrets? Yet, she obviously needed to tell someone what was bothering her. Were his past as clean as everyone thought, he would feel free to push Robin to confide in him, even to pursue her. Instead, he could only mount a subtle campaign to win the lady's trust as her pastor, though he could not technically claim even that much relationship with her.

After the midweek service, during which Robin raised her hand when he asked if there were any unspoken prayer requests, she and the three others whom he'd asked to stay for a cappella practice gathered in the front of the sanctuary. That, however, was not where he intended for them to ultimately practice or perform. Since he had hand delivered the music to everyone on Monday, they should all be familiar with it by now. One of the ladies played the piano, so she sat down to pick through the melody with chords, giving everyone the proper notes for harmony. They ran through the song once with the piano and again without it before Ethan moved them all out into the vestibule.

"Now, bear with me," he said, glancing at Robin. "I think you'll find the acoustics out here more than satisfactory."

The ladies cast doubtful looks at each other, but they stood and sang. The sound resonated with a rich, full-bodied quality. Looking at one another in surprise, they went through the song again, this time using their voices to full effect. Ethan felt the hair lift on his forearms as the music swelled and eddied around them. Giving each other congratulatory smiles, they began to realize the possibilities.

"Now, the bells," Ethan said, grinning. "Robin, since we've discussed this, will you supply the cues? I'm going to take four beats to start."

She nodded, and he hurried off, returning to the sanctuary to remove two newly polished handbells from beneath the pulpit where he'd stored them earlier. With the music spread out before him, he began to ring the bells in time with the song, just as he'd practiced earlier, alternating hands and keeping in mind the tempo that the ladies had used.

One, two, three, four, the music of the bells called out in clear, sweet tones, and the women lifted their voices as if in reply. The effect was joyous, bright but also ethereal, poignant, enough almost to bring tears to his eyes. He rang the bells again at the rests, and at the end he let them overlap the ladies' voices. They came gushing into the sanctuary, laughing, clapping and all talking at once.

"That was beautiful!"

"Amazing!"

"Could you hear us okay?"

"Perfectly," he replied to that last. "It was everything I'd hoped for."

"Imagine what everyone will say when we do this on Christmas morning."

"Won't it be lovely?"

"I can hardly wait!"

"How did you come up with this?"

"Oh, it was mostly because of Robin," Ethan answered breezily.

"It wasn't," she countered at once, glancing around. "The whole thing was your idea."

"I remembered you saying that you'd sung in college," he explained, "and it got me to thinking that we ought to have a women's group."

"So like I said, it was your idea," she pointed out doggedly. "You found the song, too."

"Yes," he agreed in a cheerful tone that belied the hurt he felt because she so obviously did not want to be too closely associated with him. "The bells," he began, merely to change the subject.

"Add a Christmassy air," she snapped.

"So they do," he replied, stung. "A very Christmassy air."

"Because otherwise," noted one of the ladies, "it's pretty much just a love song."

"Well, Christmas is the season of love, isn't it?" Ethan said, smiling limply.

"Especially around here," someone murmured.

"Good point," Ethan said, "what with the Shaw wedding on Christmas night and all." Then he clapped his hands together. "Well, I think we're done for the evening. I can go through this again on the twenty-third if that works for all of you."

They decided that would do. The music was simple, and they didn't have to memorize anything, so one more short practice should take care of things. They set a time convenient for everyone, and the group broke apart with ladies hurrying away in various directions. Robin turned to go with the others, but Ethan called her back.

"One thing, if you please, Robin."

He could see reluctance in every line of her body, and she obviously didn't like the knowing way in which the other women looked at her as they left. Still, she stayed behind. He tried to take comfort from that.

"I just want you to know that I'm never too busy for you. If you want to talk, *when* you want to talk, I'm here. I'll always be here for you."

"Oh, Ethan," she said softly, shaking her head. "You don't know what you're saying." She looked up, her big blue eyes brimming with tears. "I wish I could say the same," she choked out. "Truly I do."

With that, she hurried away.

Sighing, Ethan rubbed his forehead wearily with his hand. That could have gone better. Whatever was bothering her was clearly tearing her apart, and he couldn't bear to see it, but he couldn't help her if she wouldn't let him. All he knew to do was pray for her and hope she would confide in him.

"'But I will hope continually and praise You yet more and more,'" he quoted from the fourteenth verse of Psalm 71.

Hope. Praise. Faith. Forgiveness. Prayer. Love.

All the tools of his trade.

After he'd surrendered to the ministry, he'd thought he would be content with spiritual love. He'd never expected to find the romantic kind of love. He'd never expected to feel about a woman the way he found himself feeling about Robin Frazier, not that he had any reason to believe it would amount to anything. He didn't, given his own secrets. Still, he couldn't bring himself to ignore her pain and anxiety.

As a pastor, it was his job to help her. That being the case, he would just have to stumble forward prayerfully, hold on to hope, forget about love, leave the rest to faith and praise God for whatever came of it all.

Chapter Eight

Pageant practice the next evening was the last place Robin wanted to be, but she couldn't convince herself to shrug it off, especially as the angel and shepherd costumes were supposed to be ready for approval. With less than a week before Christmas Eve, putting off that approval would be very irresponsible. If only she didn't have to see Ethan. She couldn't trust herself around him. It was all too easy to fall into the fiction that they were becoming a couple, and she dared not let that happen, not in her dreams and especially not in reality.

Every new sunset meant that much less time left to her, the days draining away like sand in the proverbial hourglass. A subtle panic had set in. Soon she would have to leave, no matter how unbearable the thought became. She began to fear that if he simply held out his arms to her, she would find herself sobbing out the whole story against his chest. But then what?

Even if Rusty would keep her secret indefinitely, she couldn't ask Ethan, a man of God, to do so. He would loathe her lies, if not her, and she knew in her bones that he would encourage, if not insist, that she tell the truth. But how could she at this late date?

Supposing that they would even hear her out, the Shaws

were not going to believe her. Jackson would very likely hound her out of town; as the mayor and the town's leading citizen, he had the power and influence to do it. So what was the point of suffering Ethan's disdain, too? Worse, what if Ethan stood by her and Jackson decided to get rid of him, to remove him from his pastorate? It wasn't out of the realm of possibility. Jackson didn't just have a lot of clout in the community, and he also sat on the governing board of the church.

Just look at what had happened with the bridge and the bells. The Shaws had managed to close one of the only two routes into town and silence a pair of expensive, perfectly good bells for almost ninety years. What was to stop them from having Ethan stripped of his pastorate? How could she possibly live with that?

Still, Robin longed to take Ethan into her confidence, to talk it all over with him. The need had become a physical ache.

How ironic and unfair that a *pastor* should prove to be the greatest temptation she had ever faced.

Were he not a pastor, she might trust him with her secret and hope he'd be able to overlook her deceit; on the other hand, she doubted she'd find him half so attractive. Oh, the physical part wouldn't change, but that was just a fraction of what drew her. All that surfer-boy gorgeousness came with a keen, logical mind and a sweet, caring, honest personality wrapped around a strong, clean, truly good soul. He deserved a counterpart with all of the same. She hadn't been honest about why she was in town, her family connections, her great-grandmother's life and death—too much—but she tried to be a woman of her word.

So she ate a lonely dinner in her room and went to the church, arriving just as choir practice broke up. Dozens of bodies crammed the vestibule, some coming, some going. A good number of them wore white shapeless robes tied at the waist with lengths of rope. More rope formed straps for stiff wings covered in white feathers. Robin nodded approval over half a dozen similarly garbed angels before she could move forward.

She hadn't gone three steps when a young shepherd and his mother blocked her way. He wore cowboy boots with his homespun robe and a coiled length of rope over one shoulder. His mother held out two cowboy hats, a crisp natural straw and a neat black felt with a smartly steamed and shaped crown. Robin made a face.

"Don't you have anything floppy and worn?"

The woman bit her lip. "His dad might have an old gray felt work hat. It would be too big, but I could pad it inside."

"Let's do that."

She turned and found herself nose to collar button with Winston Harcourt, a rancher who lived about twenty minutes outside town.

"Red or white?" he asked. Robin backed up a step, blinking. "Chicken. You want a red or white?"

"Oh." She had to think back to the photo they'd used for the program. "Uh, red."

He nodded. Putting her head down, she stepped to one side and walked swiftly to the sanctuary door. She yanked it open to find Ethan on the other side.

"Am I ever glad to see you," he said. "Can you come take a look at the set?" He caught her hand, laced his fingers through hers and tugged her down the aisle toward the front of the church, where several men were quickly erecting the simple set.

The next hour went as the first few minutes had gone. She answered innumerable questions, approved costumes or made suggestions to bring them in line with what was expected, while Ethan gave direction and instruction. Finally they were ready for a run-through. It turned out to be more of a bumpy slog. With dress rehearsal only two days away, Robin couldn't help worrying that the whole thing was going to wind up a great fiasco.

Ethan just shrugged and announced they'd try it the next evening, Friday, with the animals. The children chattered excitedly about that, but the Shaw brothers came over to remind him that all the pageant stuff had to be cleared away and the sanctuary cleaned up right after the performance for their sister's wedding. Despite his obvious weariness, Ethan calmly assured them that they had nothing to fear.

"The sanctuary has to be clear for the Christmas-morning service. That's why we've laid hopsacking on the floor. We'll just move everything out the back, roll up the sacking and bag it, vacuum and we're done. The pulpit will remain out of sight in my office, but we'll move the altar back in."

"Marie will want in here right after the Christmas-morning service to decorate," Austin pointed out.

"No problem. I've already told your mother that Marie can store the candelabra, flowers and pew bows in the fellowship hall until they're needed. And the chairs for the musicians are stacked against the wall there."

"I guess we're good, then."

"I think we're in excellent shape," Ethan told him, slapping him on the shoulder. "Thanks for all your hard work on this. It's going to be fantastic, the pageant, the Christmas service and the wedding, too."

Nodding and smiling, Austin moved off with his brother, following the crowd. Robin sighed wearily and shook her head.

"You don't really believe that."

"I do," Ethan insisted. "It's going to be wonderful, all of it."

She goggled at him. "Ethan! Not a single person got a cue right tonight."

He waved that away. "They'll do better when it matters."

"The *sheep* stampeded."

"Their mothers will take them in hand."

"One of the angels shoved her little sister off the riser."

"But no harm was done," he said patiently. "Several people laughed."

"It was the next thing to a riot!"

"It was sweet and funny and homey," he told her. "I wouldn't change a thing."

"Nothing?" she demanded, aware that she was being strident but unable to help herself. "You wouldn't keep shepherds from sword fighting with their staffs? You wouldn't ask mothers to pipe down enough backstage so we can hear the reading? You wouldn't stop the wise men from tossing pennies while you were trying to get everyone's attention?"

"They were *spinning* pennies. They weren't gambling. Tossing pennies is gambling."

"Well, excuse me," she huffed. "If they were gambling in church, then of course we'd have to get a handle on things, but as it is, everything's perfect!"

"No, it's not perfect," Ethan declared, throwing up his hands. "If everything were perfect, my sister and niece would be here to see it all and celebrate it. You'd be smiling and laughing and not keeping secrets from me!"

Stricken, Robin felt all the fight drain out of her. Shaking her head, she did the very thing she'd feared she'd do; she walked straight into his arms.

"Oh, Ethan," she said against the strong wall of his chest. "I just want to protect you."

"From what?" he urged. "What could be so awful that I'd need protection from it?"

"Not what. Who," she whispered.

Before he could press her for more, she searched through the joy and the pain for something safe, anything that wouldn't give him an opening to force the truth from her. Two words leaped out at her: *sister* and *niece*.

My sister and niece would be here.

Lifting her head, she asked, "Why aren't your sister and niece coming?"

She expected him to say that they couldn't afford the trip or that his sister couldn't get off work or perhaps that she had other obligations.

Instead, he cut her a sharp look and morosely said, "My sister does not even speak to me, let alone spend holidays with me."

Seeing the hurt in his eyes, Robin couldn't let that pass, so when he trudged over to the front pew and plopped down, she went and sat next to him, not too close but within reach.

For a moment, she couldn't think of anything to say, but then she asked, "What's your sister's name?"

The corners of his mouth curled tightly. "Colleen. Colleen Connaught. Our mother was Irish." He slipped into an Irish brogue as easily as if the accent was a favorite T-shirt. "Mary Annette Kelly, from Dublin, where she caught the eye of one Johnny Jack Johnson, merchant marine." He shook his head, dropping the accent. "Poor woman. She thought she was heading for a better life."

"She wasn't?"

"No. Johnny Jack liked to drink. She died too young, disillusioned and lonely, longing for family and the familiar surroundings of home. She was brought up a staunch Catholic and wouldn't divorce or defy him."

"What happened? How did she die?"

"A problem pregnancy. Not her first. The doctor warned her not to become pregnant again, so she simply didn't go back to him. When she became bloated and short of breath, Colleen and I begged her to see another doctor, but she tried home remedies instead. She stroked, and we lost her and the baby."

"I'm so sorry, Ethan."

He nodded. "I was twelve. Colleen was fifteen. Dad went to pieces, so Colleen kept everything together. I'll say this for him, he might not have been a good husband, but he grieved Mom. He stayed drunk for a solid six months after her passing."

"Oh, Ethan."

"Then he sobered up and took ship again, leaving us with his older sister, Molly. She never married. Their father was an invalid from his thirties on after an accident at work, so she helped their mother take care of him, and then she took care of her mother until she died, and then she took care of us."

"Sounds like the Johnsons had a rough life," Robin ventured, aware that none of this explained why his sister didn't speak to him.

He shrugged. "No rougher than many, far less than some."

Her own life sounded like a fairy tale in comparison, and she felt more ashamed than ever for her duplicity and self-pity.

"When Colleen was nineteen," Ethan said, "Dad brought home a friend, a young Irishman named Warren Connaught. No one was surprised when Colleen and Warren married. He took her to Ireland on their honeymoon. A seagoing man like Dad, he was in and out of our lives. Colleen was crazy about him. Aunt Molly said their marriage was like being on a perpetual honeymoon—there was no reality to it. He promised to stay ashore once they had children. Colleen lost two babies before Erin was born eight years ago. True to his word, Warren gave up the sea, but he didn't want to live in the United States, so he

prepared to take Colleen and the baby to Ireland to live."
Ethan stopped and drew a deep breath.

"What happened?" Robin asked.

Ethan sat silent for so long that Robin began to think
he wouldn't answer, but then he said, "Johnny Jack happened. He threw them a going-away party. Johnny Jack
is big on parties, especially parties with lots of drinking,
and where there are sailors and drinking, there are fights."

"Oh, no."

"When the brawl broke out, Warren went to stop it, for
Colleen's sake. The baby was there after all. Dad took ex-
ception. 'What's a good party without a good fight?' he
wanted to know. He was almost too drunk to stand at that
point, but that didn't stop him from turning on his son-in-
law or picking up a bottle." Ethan paused then rushed on.
"He killed Warren with a single blow."

Gasping, Robin covered her mouth with her hand. "Poor
Colleen!"

Ethan gulped and nodded. "Because I had just started
college at the time, I didn't get there until right before the
funeral." He ran a hand over his face, gritting out, "Dad
at least had the decency to take a plea bargain and spare
the family the ordeal of a trial. He got eleven years for
manslaughter."

"I am so sorry," Robin whispered.

Ethan put his head back and closed his eyes for several
long moments before going on. "My niece, Erin, is eight
now. Dad will be up for parole soon."

"I—I don't know what to say. But…how can Colleen
blame you with any of this?"

"Oh, she doesn't," Ethan told her, leaning forward. "She
blames me for what happened three years ago."

"I don't understand."

"I had been writing to my father about his spiritual con-
dition," Ethan explained, "and he finally wrote to me that

he had accepted Christ. He asked me to bring Colleen to see him so he could beg her forgiveness." Ethan looked down at his hands. "I'm afraid I handled that rather badly. She was resistant, and I was…preachy, insistent, arrogant even. I made a mull of the whole thing, and she hasn't spoken to me since. I finally stopped trying to make her."

Robin reached out and took his hand. "Time has a way of smoothing over things. Eventually she'll come around."

"I pray so," he murmured, gripping her fingers. "I miss her. And Erin. Looking at all those angels tonight, I kept imagining Erin as one of them. You know?" He made a fist of his free hand and pounded his knee, demanding, "What sort of pastor am I if I can't even reach my own sister?"

"Don't say that," Robin scolded lightly. "Family is often the most difficult to reach. They know all our faults and foibles after all. Colleen doesn't know the Ethan I do. She remembers the brother who pulled her hair and tattled on her."

He chuckled. "Sadly, that's true." Sobering, he added, "And more besides. There were some who expected me to be my father's son in every sense of the word."

"*That* I can relate to," she said, rolling her eyes. "Ever hear of the Templeton foundation?"

He furrowed his brow, thinking. "Just the Templeton science foundation."

"That's it. The Templeton Foundation for Scientific Research."

"What about it?"

"My mother is Sheila Templeton, *Dr.* Sheila Templeton Frazier. Her grandfather established the foundation."

"Oh, wow."

"Her parents were both research scientists who worked for the foundation."

"Double wow."

"My father, Gary, now runs the foundation."

"You're putting me on."

Robin shook her head. "And I, the only Templeton heir—the only Frazier heir, for that matter—am a lowly historian."

Ethan frowned. "What's lowly about being a historian?"

"It means that I will have no role in the foundation, so it will pass out of the control of the Templeton family entirely when my parents retire."

Smiling lazily, Ethan said, "Sounds to me like Gary and Sheila should have had more than one child."

"Oh, no," Robin proclaimed, fighting back a chortle. "My mother's fifteen-year career plan allowed just two years for pregnancy and childbearing, and I took too long to conceive."

Ethan made a choking sound. "Seriously? It occurs to me," he said, "that there might be such a thing as too much soberness after all."

They both laughed.

A door closed at the back of the sanctuary, and they turned their heads, twisting on the pew and breaking apart their hands. Faith Shaw and Dale Massey stood together at the top of the center aisle, the engaged couple to wed on Christmas night. They made a striking pair, petite Faith with her lustrous auburn hair swaying about her shoulders and tall, dusky-blond Dale who, despite his casual clothing, still looked like money walking.

"Ethan," Faith said, nodding in greeting.

"You asked us to stop by," Dale reminded him.

Rising, Ethan threw out his arms in welcome. "Of course. Thank you for coming. Our last light chat before the big event."

Robin took that as her cue. More like her *rescue*. Much more of this private conversation and she'd be telling Ethan everything. As touched as she was by Ethan's taking her into his confidence, she dared not return the favor. Besides, she made it a point to avoid Faith Shaw whenever she could. She quite liked the other woman, but ever since Faith had learned that she and Robin shared the same middle name, Elaine, Robin had tried to steer clear of her. If Faith ever put together Robin's resemblance to Elaine Shaw, Jasper Gulch founder Ezra Shaw's wife and Faith's great-grandmother, with their shared middle name, she might realize they had a familial connection. If she then started to think about the fact that Lucy's body had never been recovered after the accident on the bridge, Faith and all the Shaws might start asking themselves if Robin had some connection to them, and if so, why she had kept it a secret all these months. And then they'd almost certainly come up with all the most logical but wrong conclusions.

Robin popped up and began gathering her things, addressing Ethan. "I'll see you tomorrow evening."

"This won't take long," he said. "If you don't mind waiting, we could—"

"No. No, no," she refused brightly, shouldering her bag and tucking papers under her arm. "Everything else can wait until tomorrow."

He started after her. "I should walk you out anyway."

She put out a stiff arm. "No. I insist. It's been a long day for everyone. I'm going home. You finish up and do the same."

"It has been a long one, hasn't it?" said Faith, unknowingly aiding Robin's cause.

"But just think," Dale murmured. "One week from today, we'll be married."

"Only a week," Faith said dreamily. Then she slapped her hands against her cheeks. "Only a week!"

Only a week, Robin thought grimly, hurrying from the room. Two at the most. And then it was back to being the disappointment of the Templeton Fraziers.

Better that, though, than another disappointment for dear Ethan to bear.

* * *

Watching Robin rush from the sanctuary, Ethan pasted on a smile and turned to the young couple awaiting his attention. He'd asked Faith and Dale here for a brief counseling session. Many pastors required weeks of counseling before they consented to marry a couple, but as a young, single man, Ethan didn't feel qualified to truly counsel anyone concerning marriage.

Just a couple months ago, as part of the centennial celebrations, he'd performed a mass wedding ceremony for fifty couples, including two of Faith's siblings. Julie had married Ryan Travers, and Cord had married Katie Shaw—twice, actually, as the first time had been intended only for show so that the numbers worked out for the centennial event. Fortunately, Cord had realized that he meant every word of his vows, and the two had quickly made the marriage legal. Jack and Olivia McGuire and Brody and Hannah Harcourt had also married at the Old Tyme wedding event in October. Jasper Gulch was going to have a rash of anniversaries in that month from now on.

Ethan did take his responsibilities seriously, however, and it would be remiss of him not to speak with Faith and Dale at least in passing before their wedding. Ironically, Faith's father, Jackson Shaw, had tried to kindle a romance between Ethan and his eldest daughter. Ethan wondered if that was why Robin had scampered away so quickly. Did she resent his relationship with Faith?

He mentally scoffed at the idea. Wishful thinking. First of all, Faith was engaged to marry Dale Massey. Second, while Ethan and Faith respected each other, that was as far as it went, as far as it had ever gone for either of them, and everyone in town undoubtedly knew it.

Third, and most important: Robin was not the jealous, resentful type. Robin was basically sweet natured, generous, thoughtful, helpful. In truth, he just wanted to believe that she was falling in love with him, when the exact opposite might very well be the case. No, more likely, despite her kindness, she had been disturbed by what she had learned about his family, and that was not even the worst of his secrets. He couldn't blame her. An heir of the Templetons of the Templeton Foundation for Scientific Research could do far better than him.

He didn't know why he had told Robin about his family. He hadn't intended to, but the moment had felt so right. Perhaps he had hoped that if he confided in her, she would return the favor, but it had obviously been a mistake.

Ethan had often wondered if Jackson Shaw really considered the pastor good enough for his daughter and if that opinion wouldn't change if, *when,* the truth of Ethan's past became known. Now he'd learned that Robin's mother's family was far above the Shaws, or so he imagined.

Abruptly he recognized Faith and Dale's puzzlement as they waited for him to begin, and suggested they go into his office, explaining, "I just want to be sure that you each have a good understanding of where the other is spiritually before you embark upon your married life."

"That sounds like a fine idea," Faith said, falling into step beside Dale.

"I agree," he concurred as they followed along behind Ethan. "We have talked about it, but you may have thought of something we've missed."

At least he'd gotten *that* right, Ethan mused. He silently prayed for wisdom and guidance as he counseled this young couple about to commit themselves to each other in marriage. And for the first time he asked God if he would ever have the opportunity to make that same commitment himself, if not with Robin then with someone else. Right now, he had a difficult time imagining who that might be, but he could trust God to imagine her for him.

A very short while ago, he hadn't been able to imagine himself married at all. He supposed that was progress. Even if it felt like travail.

Chapter Nine

If Thursday's practice had been somewhat disorganized, Friday's was pure chaos. Ethan tried to take joy from the small delights. The children loved the animals, Chauncey Hardman made an excellent narrator, better even than Robin or Ethan himself, and the angels and human sheep were absolutely adorable. Chauncey nearly swallowed her tongue when Lilibeth showed up sans makeup, her pretty blond hair hidden beneath a cheap black wig and a pale blue veil. The teen beauty was taking her role seriously, a fact that pleased Ethan enormously.

Nevertheless, Ethan wondered if he shouldn't have kept the Christmas pageant a small, simple production, limiting the characters to just the holy family, a shepherd or two and a single angel. So many of the children wanted to participate, however, at least according to their parents, that he'd decided to go big. Sadly, big equaled chaos.

Robin seemed to be handling it okay, though, so he tried not to stress. Thankfully, the second run-through went more smoothly, and that made him feel better about the whole thing, especially as he would finally get to show the bell ropes to Robin.

Finding a moment as everyone was leaving, he murmured in her ear, "Can you stay?"

She reached up a hand and touched that precious little flat mole right below the wing of her left eyebrow. "I, um, really don't have much time tonight. We're working so feverishly at the museum to get everything ready there, and—"

"I want to show you the ropes for the bells," he interrupted softly, knowing an excuse when he heard one.

Her blue gaze zipped to his, and she whispered, "I have a few minutes," emphasizing the word *few*.

He smiled and went to hold the side door to help Ryan Travers and Cord Shaw get the sheep out of the building, Julie Shaw Travers being the sheep rancher in this area. After that, he helped everyone else he could find, holding coats and mittens, knit caps and scarves, even the occasional handbag, while folks outfitted themselves for the chilly night and hurried away, racing to their vehicles against the blustery winds that swept down off the icy mountaintops.

Finally, only he and Robin remained, but he stalled her until he'd locked all the doors. He'd managed to keep this secret from the rest of the town so far, and he saw no reason to give up the plan now. Assured that they wouldn't be interrupted unexpectedly, he moved to the cabinet in the vestibule and removed the shelves.

Hauling out the heavy box in which the ropes with their brass fittings had come, he slid it across the stone floor. Robin went down on her knees, heedless of the damage that she might do to her slim, black knit pants, and folded back the flaps. The ropes, he had been surprised to find, were crimson, and the fittings shiny brass.

"These are beautiful."

"I know. It's a pity they won't be seen."

"Maybe you can leave the closet open after Christmas," she suggested. "Once you ring the bells, there's no reason to keep the closet closed."

"Hmm," he considered. "It would need a gate or something, though. Maybe a grille of some sort. Otherwise, I'll have kids in there yanking on the bells all the time."

"It's something to think about," she murmured, staring down at the ropes.

"I was thinking that we might try to thread and attach the ropes tomorrow morning," he told her. "I won't have many more opportunities."

"O-okay," she agreed, her tone heavy with reluctance despite the smile she attempted.

"This needs to be done near the time for the recorded carillon so we can disguise any accidental bongs," he explained, his own spirits dampened.

She looked down at the box. "I understand."

"Dress rehearsal is at four in the afternoon," he went on, "so the three o'clock carillon might be pushing it. If we go for the morning and things don't work out, we can try again at noon. What do you think?"

She nodded. "I think you're right. I'll come about eight-thirty in the morning."

"Come earlier. I'll give you breakfast," he suggested, though it sounded like pleading to his own ears.

She pushed up to her feet then bent to brush off her knees, saying, "You don't have to do that. I'll come at eight-thirty."

"Of course I don't *have* to do it," he said, irritated at her attempts to keep him at arm's length. "I *want* to do it, and I think I've made that obvious."

She sucked in a deep breath, her gaze never meeting his. "Ethan, I'm sorry, but—"

"Forget it," he snapped, more hurt than he had any right to be.

Going very still, she said nothing for several seconds. Then she gulped and quietly said, "Please don't be angry with me."

Contrite, he stepped around the box and slipped his hands down her arms to her hands, feeling the bumpy pattern of her heavy, dark green sweater beneath his fingertips. Her hands trembled in his.

"I'm not angry with you. I just worry that you're disappointed in me."

Her gaze zipped up to his. "Of course not! Why would you think such a thing?"

"Because of what I told you about my family."

"Don't be silly. That just serves to make you a better pastor."

"Then I really don't understand what's going on."

She looked down, fixing her gaze on his chest. "I know."

"Can't you help me?"

"No."

Frustration slammed into him again. "What am I going to do with you?" he asked, reaching up to curl a finger beneath her chin.

She allowed him to tip her face up but kept her gaze carefully downcast. Her words came out as less than a whisper. "There's nothing to do." Tears trickled from her big round eyes, spilling down her cheeks.

"Sweetheart, don't," he crooned, wrapping her in his arms. "I hate to see you cry."

She tried to smile. God bless her. She tried to smile for him, and the effort stabbed him straight to the heart. Groaning, he bent his head and kissed her as he'd wanted to for so long. With a sound of pure longing, she threaded her arms around his neck and leaned into him, melding her lips with his. Then suddenly she wrenched away, covering her lips with the back of her hand.

Words tumbled off his tongue, desperate, automatic words. "I'm sorry. I didn't mean to do that."

"Don't you dare apologize!" she warbled. "I can't bear it!"

"Then tell me what's wrong," he pleaded. "Just talk to me."

"I can't!" she cried, shaking her head. "I just can't."

She turned and hurried to the closet in the opposite corner, wrenching her coat from a hanger and grabbing the handbag she'd left on a shelf there. Ethan followed her.

"You need to tell me what's bothering you."

"No."

"Robin."

"Please, Ethan!" She rushed to the door, which she could have easily unlocked, but then she just stood there. *"Please."*

Reluctantly, Ethan walked over and flipped the lock. "Will you still help me with the bell ropes?"

She seemed to steel herself before replying. "Yes. But don't expect anything else."

Feeling as if he'd been punched in the gut, he watched her toss on her coat and hurry out. Then he went to safely stow away the ropes before heading back to his office to grab his laptop computer. He didn't have internet access at either the church or the parsonage. He'd had to choose between internet service and his cell phone; the cell phone had seemed more necessary, if not essential.

A couple places in town provided internet access for their customers this late at night: the Fidler Inn and the diner. It was almost closing time at Great Gulch Grub, but thankfully the lights were still on at the diner when he got there. Carrying his laptop inside, he parked himself at the closest table, ordered a piece of pie and a cup of hot decaf and went to work. It didn't take long to confirm his worst fears.

The Templeton foundation was the best-known research organization of its kind in the Southwest. Endowed by Jay Ralph Templeton to the tune of eighty-six million dollars in 1970, it had managed to triple its endowment through investments and patents while administering the original amount in grants in the first thirty years. It was expected to double both endowment and grants in the next five years, under the guidance of CEO Gary Lyle Frazier, Robin's father, who was featured in an article and photographed accepting an award.

Something about Gary Frazier struck Ethan as strangely familiar, perhaps his similarity to Robin. Then again, he didn't look all that much like his daughter except in coloring. He stood next to his wife, Dr. Sheila Carol Templeton Frazier. Oddly, she didn't look like her daughter at all except around the mouth. She was shorter and stouter, and her coloring couldn't be described as anything but mousy, while Robin had a lovely, lithe figure, not to mention those big round blue eyes and that peaches-and-cream complexion to go with her pale, wheat-blond hair.

Despite Dr. Templeton Frazier's plainness, however, she had the same look about her that Dale Massey did, the look of wealth and privilege. Suddenly, Ethan knew who Gary Frazier reminded him of: the Shaws, any Shaw, slightly more down to earth than the Masseys but somehow a step above the common folk. Just as the Masseys and Shaws were Jasper Gulch royalty, more or less, the Templetons and Fraziers were the New Mexico equivalent— only more so.

Myrtle, the middle-aged waitress, came over with his pie. "Here ya go, surfer boy. Eat quick so I can close up, will ya?"

Nodding, he picked up his fork, but then for some reason he said, "You know, Myrtle, I've only been surfing a few times in my life."

"That so?"

"My family didn't have much money, and we didn't live near the beach, and I didn't hang around with the kind of people who surfed."

"Ya still are cute, though," she told him, winking before she sauntered off, her dark curls bouncing.

Cute, he very much feared, meant less than nothing to the Templeton Fraziers, as, very likely, did the collar that he wore in the pulpit. What, if anything, would it mean to Robin once she knew the whole truth about him? Suddenly, he couldn't have eaten that pie if his life had depended on it. He put down his fork and bowed his head.

Her mouth full of toothpaste, Robin seriously considered not answering the phone when it rang less than twenty minutes after she got back to her room. If Ethan was calling, she'd just cry again. If her mother was on the phone, Robin would have to pretend that all was well when it wasn't. If Olivia was ringing, Robin would be working tomorrow in addition to everything else, but maybe that wasn't such a bad thing. She spat and rushed out to snatch up the receiver.

"Hello."

"Hi, Robin."

She had not expected to hear her father's voice.

"Can you hang on a minute, Daddy? I'll be right back."

She dropped the receiver onto the bed before walking slowly into the bathroom. Why would her father be calling? In many ways, she felt closer to him than to her mother, but he usually let Sheila take care of the communication end of things, especially since Robin had come to Jasper Gulch against his express wishes. She rinsed and returned to sit on the side of the bed. Gingerly, she lifted the telephone receiver to her ear again.

"Sorry. I was brushing my teeth when you called."

"Didn't mean to interrupt. We just haven't talked in a while."

Robin had twisted her hair up out of her way. It wobbled as she leaned back against the headboard of the bed.

"I've been busy. The museum here opens on New Year's Eve, and we have nearly three dozen displays to get ready."

"Is that why you aren't coming home for Christmas?" he asked.

"Partly."

"And the other part?"

"I'm involved in a bunch of stuff at church."

"At church," he echoed. "Sounds like you're really settling in there."

She wanted to settle in, but that didn't seem possible now. An ache started in her chest and moved up into her throat. She tried to clear it away with a cough.

"Not so much as you might think, actually. It, um, sort of has to do with my job here and the centennial."

"Speaking of jobs," he said. "I thought we ought to get some things straight about that." He went on to tell her that her mother might have mischaracterized the position that would shortly become available for funding. It was not a pure science position but a position researching grants, studies, corresponding data, fellowships and even individuals. "I know it sounds dry," he went on, "but some of it is actually very interesting, and it keeps us from repeating the same studies over and over. It's useful work, essential for the foundation, really, and it pays well. We've just installed some new cross-referencing software that is state-of-the-art, and you would get to decide who could access it for what purposes. It's a researcher's dream, really."

"I see," she said, trying to keep tears at bay. Was this God's solution to her dilemma?

"Besides," her father added, "we want you home. We miss you."

"I miss you, too," she said, and to her surprise found that it was true. But, oh, how she would miss Jasper Gulch—and Ethan—when she left here.

"You'll think about the job, then?" Gary asked.

"I'll think about it," she promised, knowing already that she would take it, that she likely had little choice in the matter. She could hear her father's smile.

"That's great. That's just great."

He asked about her plans for Christmas, and she realized to her dismay that she really didn't have any beyond the pageant and the Christmas-morning service. Shoving aside those thoughts for the time being, she put on a brave front and launched into a recitation about the centennial Christmas that she had helped Ethan plan for the church. Without once actually mentioning Ethan's name, she described the decorations, the Hanging of the Green service, the pageant, the planned Christmas-morning service, even the printed programs and the a cappella quartet. She left out the bells; that secret belonged to her and Ethan alone, at least until they shared it with the church and town.

"What about the Shaws?" her father asked when at last she wound down.

"Oh, them," she said in as offhand a manner as she could manage. "Their eldest daughter is getting married on Christmas night. They're all wrapped up in that. I don't imagine they have time for a distant cousin who won't be hanging around much longer anyway."

"Well, I'm glad you got that out of your system," he told her, not bothering to hide his relief. "Look, I know we're short on family," he said, "but one day you'll meet a nice young man and start a family of your own. Then it won't matter. You'll see."

Will I? she wondered. *Or have I already met him and ruined it all with my lies?*

They chatted a few minutes longer, then hung up. Robin felt both better and worse. She thought she could survive leaving town without the Shaws knowing who and what she was. She could get along with just the little bit of family she had; she'd done so to this point. Even the job that her parents were holding open for her didn't sound too bad. If it paid the bills and pleased her parents, she could always find ways to indulge her interest in history. She would miss her friends, but she'd lost friends before and survived. Perhaps if she left town, Rusty wouldn't tell what he knew, and the truth about the accident on the bridge would remain hidden. The bridge was being rebuilt after all, and what good would it do to reopen old wounds? If her great-grandmother could live with that lie, Robin supposed she could, too.

What cut her to the quick, what killed her, was the idea of never seeing Ethan again, of never knowing how he fared, what he needed, who helped him, if he made peace with his sister and got to see his niece and aunt again. To think that he had family from whom he was estranged pained Robin, not only because she identified with his need for family, but also because she knew it pained him so very deeply. If she could give him one thing before she left, it would be what she herself could not have: family.

And why not? she wondered. Maybe it was none of her business, but he could hardly hate her more than he was going to anyway. Why shouldn't she try to fix things between him and his sister? What her father had said about cross-referencing had gotten her to thinking about how she could find Ethan's family.

Recalling all that he'd told her, Robin pulled out a pad of paper and a pen and began making notes. His aunt's name was Molly Johnson. His sister's name was Colleen Connaught. They lived in the Los Angeles area of California. All she had to do was find a Molly Johnson and a Colleen Connaught with the same address in the environs of Los Angeles. Shouldn't be too difficult. Might take some time, though, and she didn't want to use the computers at the museum for the search, not that she had much time at work right now for anything but putting together exhibits.

She retrieved her tablet from her bag and logged onto the Wi-Fi provided by the inn. By the time she collapsed into bed two hours later, she'd succeeded only in eliminating all the Molly Johnsons in Los Angeles proper, by virtue of the fact that no Colleen Connaught cross-referenced with any of them, and making a list of the dozens of smaller towns that comprised the greater Los Angeles area, but she wasn't going to give up. She was going to find Ethan's sister and speak to her before she left this town, hopefully before Christmas.

Her alarm woke her at seven-thirty. She showered, then gulped down a cup of coffee and frozen pastries heated in the microwave before blowing dry her hair and outfitting herself for another cold day. Choosing warmth and comfort over style, she caught her hair in a ponytail low on the back of her head, slipped on a wide, thick, navy blue knit headband and stepped into her oldest jeans, which she paired with a snug brown rib-knit sweater. To this she added her hiking boots and down-filled coat. The sun shined bright out of a clear blue sky, so she donned a pair of sunglasses as she went out the door, the strap of her bag over her shoulder.

She arrived at the church a few minutes early, but she'd hardly put the transmission into Park before she spied Ethan via her side-view mirror, coming out the front door of the parsonage. Slinging on his coat, a piece of toast in his teeth, he ran across the street. She let herself out of the car in time to meet him as he arrived. He swallowed what he was chewing and tossed aside the remainder of his breakfast, dusting off his face and hands.

"Thank you for coming."

"I told you I would."

"I know. I didn't doubt it." He huffed out a deep breath, fogging the air. "But I realize you'd rather not."

She reached up to remove her sunglasses. "That isn't so."

"Are you sure? I know you say you aren't put off by what I told you about my father, but some think the apple doesn't fall far from the tree. That's why you're the only one here I've told."

Touched, she smiled at him. "You don't have to worry that I'll tell anyone else."

"I don't," he said, "and not because you're good at keeping secrets. I intend to reveal all of mine, just gradually."

Frowning, she leaned back against the car door and looked down at her toes. "Sometimes there seems no point in revealing secrets."

"Why? Become some might disapprove? I can't imagine your parents, for instance, would approve of someone who has close family serving time in prison."

"They don't approve of *me*," she reminded him. That might change, though, if she returned home, took the job. *When,* she reminded herself. *When* she returned home and took the job at the foundation.

She realized suddenly that the job her father had pitched last night was not the same job her mother had pressed her on before. One had been funded through Templeton at the university; her dad had essentially offered her a spot at the foundation itself. This went beyond a simple "mischaracterization." This was her big "in," a tailor-made position to fold her into the bosom of her family, the only family she truly had. Perhaps she should be thrilled about that, instead of desperate to avoid thinking about it.

She glanced pointedly at her watch, saying, "We ought to get busy."

Ethan raised his hand, and she preceded him up onto the boardwalk. As they drew near the front door of the church, he slid around her, pulling his keys from his coat pocket. He unlocked the door and let her inside, reaching around her to flip on lights. Stepping in behind her, he closed and locked the door. The stone antechamber felt chilly despite the low hum of the central-air unit, but they quickly went to work removing the shelves and getting out the ropes, which they stretched across the vestibule. He held up a long, blunt wooden dowel with a metal ring screwed into one end.

"This," he said, "is apparently a thread needle. We attach the clip on one end of the rope to the ring, push the needle through the eye in the wall in the closet there and pull the rope through up top. Then I detach the clip from the needle and attach it to the arm of one of the bells."

"And we repeat the process with the other rope."

"Exactly."

He opened the trapdoor, pulled down the ladder and, after donning a cap and gloves, climbed up into the belfry. When he gave the order, Robin lifted the ladder and closed the trap, then hurried into the closet to push the rope through the eye as he pulled. While she waited for him to send the thread needle back down, her cell phone rang. She tugged off her gloves and answered the call.

It was Olivia, wondering if Robin could meet her at the museum to work for a while. With only ten days left before the opening and Christmas smack in the middle, time was short.

"Uh, sure," Robin told her, "but I have to be at the church by four for dress rehearsal, and it might take me some time to get over to the museum."

"It's okay," Olivia assured her. "I'm not ready to head into town yet myself, and I'll take whatever help you can give me. I'll text when I get to the museum, and you can come over then."

"Deal."

Just as she rang off, Ethan called through the closed trapdoor. "One down and one to go. Open the trap."

She did so, and he dropped the wooden dowel, watching as she hurried over to pick it up and clip on the rope.

She closed the trapdoor again then moved back into the closet. Pushing the thread needle through the eye proved more difficult the second time, partly because one side of the channel in the center of the eye was already filled with rope and partly because the second channel was on top of the eye. She had to stack up some hymnals on which to stand in order to force the long wooden needle through the space. Finally, she heard Ethan shout that he had it.

She returned the hymnals, put the box in which the ropes had been shipped back into the closet and waited for Ethan to tell her to open the trap so he could come down. It was almost nine before he stepped off the ladder onto the floor of the vestibule again.

"Quick," he told her, hurrying for the closet as the carillon began to play.

She used the pole to push up the ladder and close the trapdoor. Suddenly, the whole room seemed to vibrate with the deep resonance of the bells overhead. Running to the closet, she found Ethan with one leg braced against the wall as he pulled first one rope and then the other, his face alight with joy.

"This is definitely a two-person job!" he shouted, obviously laboring.

She laughed. "So I see!"

To stop the bells from ringing, he wound the ropes securely around the anchors bolted into the rock wall and stepped out of the closet, throwing his arms wide. "We did it, Robin. We roped the bells. And we're going to ring them for Christmas," he vowed, grinning broadly.

"Everyone's going to be so surprised," she enthused, clapping her hands.

"And pleased, I hope."

"I'm sure of it."

Reaching out, he looped his gloved hands around her

neck and pulled her to him, dropping his forehead to hers. "Thank you. Again. For everything."

She shook her head, rubbing her forehead against his, her heart full to the point of bursting. "It's been my pleasure, all of it."

Her phone beeped, letting her know that she'd received a text. Taking full advantage of the interruption, she jerked away, whipping the little technological wonder from her pocket.

"I have to go. Olivia needs me."

Sighing, Ethan waved a hand. "Go. Go. But I'll see you at four. Right?"

"At four," she promised, beating a hasty retreat.

Saved by the beep.

After the bells.

She couldn't even get her metaphors right, she thought grimly, but at least she hadn't made a fool of herself, though with Ethan that was increasingly a near thing.

Chapter Ten

"**W**hose idea was this log cabin?" Livvie grumbled as she shoved at the stump beside the back wall of the small structure that took pride of place in the center of the museum gallery. The preserved stump had been placed picturesquely, the blade of an ax affixed into a precisely carved cut in its top.

"You know it was Mayor Shaw's," Robin muttered, applying an aging compound to the hewn ends of the small logs. A construction crew had erected the structure to Olivia's specifications. Now she and Olivia were dressing it for display. "That's why the plaque says that he and his wife endowed the exhibit."

"It does make an interesting focal point," Olivia conceded, sprinkling dirt over the tracks she'd made.

A pot of faux beans hung over the faux blaze in the rock fireplace inside, visible through the open door, while a seasonally appropriate pair of hares waited on the porch for skinning and cleaning. In spring they would trade the hare for fish and add onions and field greens. Summer would see berries, potatoes and larger game rotated into the display. Autumn would provide the greatest bounty. They'd set up smoking racks in the "yard" to show how meat had been processed for storage. Except Robin wouldn't be here to assist Olivia with any of those displays.

She wouldn't know what Christmas was like in Jasper Gulch next year either, or the Fourth of July, for that matter. She would never see this valley at normal, after the six-month-long centennial celebration had concluded, the bridge was reopened and life had gotten back to its everyday cadence. She would only ever have these months and this time of the centennial.

Robin stopped what she was doing and looked around her at the displays in their glass cases. Here unfolded the history of Jasper Gulch, Montana, from its earliest settlement to its founding through the following century to today. Just over nine hundred souls called this little stopover home, yet it bore a proud and noble heritage, sheltered by the surrounding mountains, its roots sinking deep into the valley floor. She was shocked to realize that the city of Albuquerque alone contained a population of well over half a million people, while the whole state of Montana, the fourth-largest in the United States by area, boasted barely more than a million, and every one of them hardy, determined, independent and, at the same time, neighborly in every sense of the word. She'd come to Montana to find family, but Montana *was* family, one big, far-flung, let-me-give-you-a-hand family. And she was leaving it all behind her.

It had taken a concerted effort to mess up things this badly, but she'd managed it.

Not a single person in this town deserved the dishonesty she had dished out since her arrival, nor the cowardly retreat she planned. Olivia, who had befriended and hired her, didn't deserve it. Rusty, who had kept her secret and tried to help her, didn't deserve it. The parents and children and performers in the pageant didn't deserve it. The ladies on the decorating and costume committees didn't deserve

it. The women in the a cappella quartet didn't deserve it.
Mamie Fidler, who had been almost a second mother to
her, certainly did not deserve such treatment from Robin.
Even the Shaws, who had shown her nothing but respect
and kindness, did not deserve to be lied to, tricked and ultimately dismissed for her pride's sake.

Most of all, Ethan did not deserve to be treated the
way she was treating him. He deserved every consider-
ation, all honesty, every bit of support she could give him
and all the happiness this world could provide. To think
that he'd worried she would look down on him because
of something his father had done made her feel small and
unworthy. He deserved the truth from her, and she deserved whatever came after that. Her pride had no say in
the matter anymore.

Robin finished up what she was doing, then put away
her tools before checking the time. Almost fifty minutes
before she had to return to the church.

"Liv, do you mind if I call it a day? I have something
to do before dress rehearsal."

Dusting off her hands, Olivia smiled. "Oh, sure, hon.
I've kept you long enough."

"Thanks."

Robin hurried into her outer layer of cold-weather gear,
but as soon as she got into the car, she tugged off her gloves
and put in a call on her cell phone. As usual, she got her
father's voice mail, so she left a message.

"Dad, I need a favor, and I need it ASAP. That state-
of-the-art software you've had installed, will it cross-
reference addresses? If so, I need to find two women who
live at the same address in the Los Angeles, California,
area. Their names are Molly Johnson and Colleen Connaught. You'll have to try every spelling of the second
name. And please, get back to me as quickly as you can,
but not on this phone. Call the inn. Thanks. I owe you."

She couldn't take a chance that he'd call while she was with Ethan and ruin the surprise she was planning. Besides, if this didn't work, she didn't want to get Ethan's hopes up for nothing.

Back at the inn, she set about garbing herself for the dress rehearsal. The long dress with its high neckline, gathered skirt and long sleeves was not actually wool so wouldn't scratch, but she wore a black leotard under it anyway. The bodysuit gave her added warmth and doubled for stockings. Over the dress went the knee-length white smock with its gigantic floppy red bow. She twisted her hair into an adequate knot, being sure to cover her ears, and wore her plainest pumps. She'd hoped to borrow a pair of historically accurate shoes from the museum, but women of that era had proved to have ridiculously tiny feet, at least those whose shoes they had acquired anyway.

She was in the process of fixing holly in her hair when the phone in her room rang. Dropping everything into the sink, she ran to answer. It was not her father but a Templeton foundation research fellow named Abel Goodenour.

Abel spoke with a slight German accent when he said, "Greetings, Ms. Frazier. Your father has instructed me to call you with the following findings."

He went on to tell her that a Molly Johnson and a Colleen Connaught lived at a certain address in Valinda, California. He gave her the address and three phone numbers, all of which she wrote down.

"Thank you, Mr. Goodenour."

"*Dr.* Goodenour," he corrected her.

"Thank you, Dr. Goodenour," she corrected, determinedly *not* rolling her eyes. "I appreciate the information very much."

He rang off with a terse "Goodbye."

Robin could hardly contain her excitement. Perhaps soon she could speak to Ethan's sister. She wouldn't expect too much. It would be enough if Colleen would just call Ethan to wish him a merry Christmas. That and the truth were all Robin had to give him.

Everyone looked great. Ethan couldn't have been more pleased with the costumes. Unfortunately, the rehearsal could only be described as disastrous. The donkey stepped on an angel's foot, which, thankfully, did not appear to be broken despite copious tears. A sheep ran amok, much to the screaming delight of the children. The chicken tried to roost in the Christmas tree in the vestibule, which toppled and had to be put back into place. The shepherd with the rope decided to practice lassoing everyone and everything as soon as his mom was called away by the babysitter to pick up his sister, who was suspected of having a stomach virus.

"That's all we need," Chauncey Hardman exclaimed, sure that the stomach virus would run rampant through the cast and church by Christmas.

Feeling defeated, Ethan pinched the bridge of his nose, gathered everyone for prayer, then sent them all home. They knew what to do and when to do it. More practice was not going to change anything for the better; it was just going to frustrate those who took this seriously, himself included, and give more opportunity to those tending toward mischief.

The Shaws helped move the altar and pulpit to places down in front of the stage set for the next day's service. Ethan hoped that seeing the set on Sunday morning would encourage everyone to return for the Christmas Eve program, but he felt discouraged about the whole venture, or perhaps he just felt discouraged in general.

The euphoria over roping the bells that morning had vanished with Robin's eagerness to get away from him. She had as much as admitted that his concerns about her

family approving of him were merited. Worse, she'd inti-
mated that her secrets were more dire than he had antici-
pated. How they could be worse than his own, however,
he could not imagine.

Nevertheless, her fear of the truth made him fear it, not
that he would shrink from it—or so he told himself until
he realized that, for once, Robin did not have to be coaxed
to stay behind when the others left. He just looked around
as he was turning off lights and there she sat, a lone figure
in a black leotard, a great green cardigan that swallowed
her from neck to knees and an incongruous pair of brown
pumps, her costume in a plastic bag that draped, clothes
hanger down, over the back of the pew beside her.

Something in the way she sat there watching him put
his senses on alert and turned his stomach into a jumble.
They'd hardly had a chance to speak at all that evening,
but now that he thought about it, he realized that she'd been
unusually quiet and thoughtful, even for her.

He'd gotten all the lights in the sanctuary except one.
That left just the light in the vestibule and a light behind
the set, which he'd intended to switch off after checking
the side doors. Despite the golden glow of the windows
from the light poles on either side of the building, large
rectangular shadows reached across the pews, meeting in
the center aisle and banding the great hall in thick stripes
of black.

She sat calmly in a wash of muddy gold light, waiting
for him to come to her. He'd left his own smock and bow
on a hanger draped over his reading stool but wore his
tweed pants, white shirt and suspenders with an old pair
of black lace-up dress shoes. He'd parted his hair in the
middle like the parson in the old photo and slicked it down
with water, but it wouldn't stay in place.

"I have some styling gel you can use," she told him as

he nervously attempted to right the mess his hair had no doubt become, sliding his hands through it.

"Rusty told me to oil it."

"Rusty would probably know," she said with a nod. "He knows a lot. For instance, he knows all my secrets."

Ethan felt as if he'd been felled with an ax. He practically toppled into the pew beside her. "What does Rusty know?"

"First, you need to understand that I didn't tell him," she said urgently. "He guessed, and, well, he's part of it, in a way."

Confused, Ethan glanced around the shadowed space, taking in the jumbled set, the altar and the pulpit. "I don't know why I'm so surprised. It's just... We came here about the same time, you and I, and you're keeping secrets with one of the town's most respected citizens, while I feel I've barely made a start."

"But it's a good start."

"Is it?" he asked. "The truth is, I'm not much of a minister. I have my own secrets that you know nothing about. Why, my own sister won't speak to me."

"She'll come around."

"I can't see my own niece."

"You will."

"My father is in prison."

"Not because of anything you've done, and you were able to reach him, turn him to God."

"I can't take credit for that. Prison is a mighty influence on a man."

"But you didn't give up on him," she argued.

"How could I?" he asked. "God didn't give up on me. I just don't know if I'm living up to His expectations, His purpose for me."

She clasped both of his hands in hers, saying urgently,

"Now, you listen to me. You're making a difference here in this valley, Ethan Johnson."

He wanted to believe that, and he blessed her for saying so, but he had to wonder.

"Am I? Am I really? Then why don't you trust me enough to tell me your secrets?"

"I do." She bit her lip. "I just don't want you to think less of me."

Letting go of her hands, he smoothed the hair around her face, saying, "I think the world and all of you, Robin Frazier, more than I want to, to tell you the bald truth. But I can't help you if you won't tell me what's bothering you."

Sighing, she slumped against the pew and closed her eyes. Ethan let his hands fall away, but then she straightened and swiveled to face him, her knees bumping his.

"You can't help me," she said, "but I'll tell you. It all started when my great-grandmother was dying. Everyone expected it. She was one hundred and three years old, but we were very close, she and I. She wasn't gone yet, and I was already missing her, so she told me what no one had ever suspected, that her name wasn't really Lillian. It was Lucy. Lucy Shaw."

Ethan blinked at that, sure he'd misheard. "I thought you said Lucy Shaw. But that wouldn't be possible. Lucy Shaw…"

The implications slowly dawned on him.

"She didn't die when Ezra's Model T went off the bridge," Robin confirmed.

"That is wild!"

"She faked her death. So she could marry my great-grandpa Cyrus."

Ethan had a difficult time getting his teeth to meet. "Faked her death."

"Ezra wanted her to marry someone else. Rusty thinks it was to save the bank after Silas Massey left town."

"Rusty thinks?"

"He was there that night when they faked the accident, and he's kept her secret all these years."

Astonished, Ethan leaned forward, braced his elbows on his knees and rubbed his hands over his face, trying to wrap his mind around this information. "Lucy didn't die, and Rusty has known it all along. She was your great-grandmother and told you all this on her deathbed, so…" He sat up straight. "You're kin to the Shaws."

Robin grimaced. "That's why I'm here. Great-Grandma wanted me to connect with my Montana family, but my parents thought it was all a hallucination on her part, and by the time I could prove she'd been telling the truth, I'd been here long enough to realize that the Shaws wouldn't take kindly to this information or my delay in bringing it to light. I mean, they are sort of the first family around Jasper Gulch. To them, I would be just a hanger-on trying to worm my way into the family for some nefarious reason."

"But you're a Templeton on your mother's side," Ethan pointed out, "and my impression is that the Templetons can hold their own with the Shaws status-wise. Perhaps even eclipse them."

"Well, my mother certainly thinks so, and that's part of the problem. I've been befriended for my connections with the Templetons enough to know how unwelcome hangers-on can be, and when you add in the Masseys and the gold…"

Ethan shook his head. "The Masseys I get, sort of, with Faith marrying into that family and them being ridiculously wealthy, but what's this about gold?"

Robin rose, turned and leaned back against the pew behind her. "Rusty claims that Lucy told him the time capsule contained a fortune in gold meant for the heirs of the Shaws and the Masseys."

Ethan blew out a long breath, then, sitting back and

crossing his arms, he considered. "But when the time capsule turned up, it only contained historical documents and old photos and mementos."

"Exactly."

"So you think whoever stole the time capsule took it for the gold."

"And that had to be someone who *knew* about the gold."

"Hmm. Well, that probably means one of the Masseys or the Shaws, and that most likely means…" Ethan looked up suddenly. "You think Jackson Shaw took that gold!"

"Rusty does," Robin confirmed, "and it makes sense. Jackson could have taken it either to try to prevent the bridge from reopening or to keep the Masseys from getting their share of it because Silas *did* actually loot the bank before he left town, and the Shaws had to make good for that."

"Or for both reasons," Ethan mused.

"So you see why I'm reluctant now to tell the Shaws that we're related."

"You're afraid they'll think you're just after your share of the gold."

"Wouldn't you think so?"

"Not after I got to know you, and they all know you by now, Robin."

"Jackson doesn't! Not really. None of them do. They just *think* they do, but when they find out that I haven't been honest with them, you can see what conclusions they'll draw."

Ethan spread his hands. "Look, you don't know that Jackson took the gold. It could have been Pete Daniels like everyone suspects. Or someone no one suspects. And even if you're right about Jackson, you could just refuse any part of the gold."

"I can't do that! I'm not supposed to even know about the gold. No one is."

Ethan threw up his hands. "What a mess!"

"I know," Robin agreed, "and the worst part is that if Jackson believes I'm trying to horn in on the gold, he might decide to force me out of town."

Ethan shot to his feet. "Now, wait a minute."

"He could. You know he could."

"We won't let that happen," Ethan promised. "I know he's used to getting his own way, and he has lots of influence around here, but he can be reasoned with. I've had plenty of dealings with him already, and I—"

"No." She put out an unsteady hand, saying, "If he can do it to me, he can do it to you, too."

Ethan felt as if a shaft of sunlight had pierced his chest. "You sweetheart. You said it, but I didn't understand. That's why you didn't want to tell me. You're trying to protect me!"

She blinked rapidly, her hand sneaking up to press a fingertip against that little spot beneath her eyebrow. "Mostly I was afraid you'd be disappointed in me," she confessed.

"Disappointed?"

"I lied. All these months, I've been living a lie. I didn't come to town to write about genealogy. I came to prove my great-grandmother's story and meet my Montana family."

"And you thought I'd condemn you for that? How could I possibly when everything you've done has shown me that you're the dearest, sweetest, kindest, most caring, generous—"

She lurched forward and kissed him, pressing her lips to his. He slid his hands around the slender curve of her waist, smiling against her lips and feeling her arms creep around him.

Breaking the kiss, he rocked her gently side to side and laid his nose against hers, whispering, "We are a pair, you and I, with our secrets and our fears."

"I'm so glad I told you," she said, "but it doesn't change anything, you know."

"Oh, but it does," he told her. "The truth always changes us, Robin. The Bible says it sets us free. Of our fears, if nothing else."

"I'm sure that's true," she agreed, pulling away to trail a hand over the back of the pew in front of them, "but I can't see any way for this to end with me staying in Jasper Gulch."

"Don't say that," he pleaded.

"It's true, though, Ethan," she argued. "I've thought and thought, and I've prayed and prayed, and no matter how I look at this, I don't see Jackson Shaw welcoming me into the family. I don't have the kind of proof that would stand up in a court of law, and I'm afraid that's what it would take for him."

Ethan couldn't dispute that. "He's a proud man but a Christian."

"His family is more important to him than even this town," Robin pointed out, "and he's been mayor here practically his whole adult life."

"But you're not a threat to his family."

"Ethan, he's fought against reopening the bridge all these years because he believes Lucy died going off it in a car accident. Do you really believe he'll consider my story as anything other than a threat to the very fabric of the family history? My delay in coming forward and the gold just give him more reason to believe that."

"So what do you propose to do?" Ethan wanted to know. "Live with the lie? I can tell you from experience that it isn't easy to do."

She shook her head. "I don't think I could. Not here anyway. How could I see Faith and Julie and Cord and the others every day, knowing we're kin, and keep a secret this big? The way I see it, I either leave without saying anything, or I tell them, they reject everything I have to say and me along with it and then I go. But either way, I'll be headed back to New Mexico by the first of the year."

"Or they could believe you," Ethan proposed hopefully.

"You know that isn't likely."

"Say they don't believe you, then," he pressed. "That doesn't mean you have to go. I agree that Jackson might try to force you out if only to quash your story, but that doesn't mean he will or that he can. Stand your ground. Tell them the truth, then stay and fight for it. Rusty will back you. You know he will."

"And what about you?" she asked, smiling softly. "Will you stand with me, Ethan?"

He clasped her hand in his. "Of course I will! It goes without saying."

To his dismay, she pulled free. "All the more reason to go. I won't let Jackson hurt you. I know how much you love it here. You told me that day up at Gazebo. Remember?"

He remembered, and he wished he could have the words back now.

"That's not important."

"Of course it is. I'm not so worried about Rusty. What can Jackson really take from Rusty? But you…you could lose your pastorate over this and have to leave Jasper Gulch. I won't let you lose your church and your home, not because of me."

She pushed past him into the aisle, snagged her costume by the hanger and started for the door. He could see that it wouldn't do any good to argue with her about this, not now, but he couldn't let her go just yet, either.

"Robin, wait!" he called, hurrying to catch up to her. "I haven't thanked you."

"For what?" she asked, letting him turn her to face him.

"For trusting me with your secret. It means more to me than you know."

Smiling, she lifted a hand to his cheek. "Good night, Ethan, and merry Christmas."

He looped his arms around her and pulled her in for a hug, laying his cheek against her crown. "Merry Christmas. Don't give up hope. I'll be praying about this whole matter."

Oh, would he pray. He'd pray that God would give her wisdom and courage. He'd pray that the Shaws would know the truth when they heard it. He'd pray that she would at last be able to claim the family for which she so obviously longed. He'd pray that Jackson's conscience wouldn't let him do the wrong thing. Mostly, though, he'd pray that God would make a way for her to stay in Jasper Gulch, long enough at least for Ethan to confess all she needed to know about him.

He wouldn't ask that she open her heart to him or that her family somehow approve of a minister who'd come from the wrong side of the tracks in L.A. He asked only that he be able to repay her trust in kind. Because anything else was simply unthinkable now.

Meanwhile, it was time he got serious about revealing his true self to his own congregation. The results of that he would leave entirely to God. It wasn't up to Jackson Shaw how long or short a time Ethan spent in Jasper Gulch. That was God's call alone, and somehow Ethan had to make Robin understand that elemental truth about his calling—one he himself had been in danger of forgetting until God had brought a certain wonderful young lady into his life.

Chapter Eleven

That Sunday, Ethan used the text about Joseph and Mary
fleeing into Egypt with the newborn baby Jesus to talk
about second chances. He compared Herod's slaughter
of male children in an effort to kill the foretold Hebrew
king to the gang violence in his own old Los Angeles–
area neighborhood. He talked about how common it was
for his neighbors and classmates to have family members
in jail. Then he admitted that he'd counted himself fortu-
nate not to be among them, only to have his father wind
up in prison for manslaughter while he was away in college. He didn't mention Colleen or that his brother-in-law
had been his father's victim. He did freely admit that only
the influence of a tough, seasoned pastor had saved him,
Ethan, from the streets and guided him to a better way of
life. Ethan then contrasted his own "moment of calling"
to Joseph being warned in a dream.

"God still speaks to us," he proclaimed, "in ways both
big and small. You have but to listen and to want to hear
what He actually has to say. Too often," he pointed out,
"we only hear what we want to hear, and then we have the
audacity to say that God no longer speaks."

Robin, at least, seemed visibly moved, but then, she
already knew the story. She came at once to his side after

the sermon, taking a place next to him at the back of the sanctuary. The McGuires were right behind her.

"You're not just a surfer boy after all," Mick McGuire said as he pumped Ethan's hand.

"Not much of a surfer *at* all, in fact," Ethan replied.

"First-rate preacher, though," Mick stated, moving off with a grin.

Jack reached past Olivia to offer his own hand, saying, "I'll second that."

"Thanks, Jack."

"That wasn't the typical Sunday-before-Christmas sermon, though," Olivia said, lifting her eyebrows.

"But a fine one," Jack insisted. "I knew there was depth to you, Ethan. I just didn't know how much."

"More than you may suspect," Ethan warned, still smiling as the McGuires filed past on their way out of the sanctuary.

"Enough, I'll warrant, to make you stick around and do well in these parts," said another, all-too-familiar voice. Beside him, Ethan felt Robin cringe as she faced the Shaws.

"Thank you, Mr. Mayor," Ethan returned easily. "That's a welcome vote of confidence."

"We like our pastors with bottom," Jackson said in his hearty baritone. "No one wants a pastor without a firm foundation beneath him." Standing an inch or so taller than Ethan's own six feet, the mayor cut an imposing figure. Broad-shouldered and long-limbed, he'd have been barrel-chested with just a little more weight. His wavy dark brown hair showed silver at the temples in deference to his sixty-some years, but his pale blue eyes held all the steel of a much younger man. "You'll do," he told Ethan, his gaze gliding over Robin with interest.

Ethan wrapped an arm around her waist and squeezed

encouragingly. To his surprise, he felt her square her shoulders.

An instant later, she stepped out of his embrace and said, "Mayor Shaw, would it be possible for me to meet with you, your wife and children this afternoon?"

Ethan caught his breath. Had she finally decided to tell the Shaws why she had come to Jasper Gulch?

Jackson seemed taken aback. "Well, I…" He looked to his wife, Nadine.

"Of course," Nadine said, putting on a polite smile. "But if this is about the wedding decorations, we're fine with everything but the pageant set."

"Uh, actually this is sort of a…historical issue," Robin hedged.

Ethan sent up a silent prayer of praise as the Shaws exchanged glances.

"You need the family for that?" Jackson asked. "Isn't that more of a museum issue?"

"Um, well, the Shaws are integral to the situation, you see," Robin said, gulping. "It's, ah, difficult to explain, but I'll try to be brief."

Jackson shrugged and said, "Might as well come for dinner."

"Oh, no." Robin shook her head. "I couldn't possibly."

"Can you come about two-thirty or three, then?" Nadine asked. "That should give us time to finish up and clear away, but any later than that and everyone will scatter."

"Before three," Robin answered.

"See you then," the mayor said, offering his arm to Nadine.

They walked off, their heads together.

Ethan reached out and squeezed Robin's hand. She stood beside him as he greeted several more people. Every comment about the sermon was positive, and he thanked God for them, even as he felt Robin drawing up tighter and tighter beside him. Oh, if only her own attempt at revelation would work out so well.

Sensing her turmoil, Ethan squeezed her hand. "Help me close up," he said, "then you can join me for Sunday dinner. Unless you have other plans."

"That would be most welcome," she admitted. "Otherwise I fear I'll lose my nerve."

"For what it's worth," he told her, "I think you're doing the right thing."

"Bless you for saying so."

"I hope you'll bless me still if the roast beef is shriveled into blackened hockey pucks," he joked. *Or if the Shaws do not welcome you into the family.*

Chuckling, she moved away to switch off lights. He went to start locking doors and pray that her joy would far surpass his before all was said and done.

Within a quarter hour they were bundling into their outerwear. Leaving her hybrid in the church parking lot, they simply walked over to the neat little white bungalow that was the parsonage. Guessing that it was built in the early 1940s, Robin took in the deep front porch across the front, the multipaned door standing between two large windows and the dormer window upstairs that overlooked the front yard.

Ethan surprised her by walking up the steps and across the porch to turn the knob on a door that he'd clearly left unlocked. Robin blinked at that.

"What?" he asked. "This is Jasper Gulch, and I don't have much worth taking anyway."

"But you're so careful to lock up the church."

"That's different. That's God's house. It can't be left to unthinking vandals. Besides, I've been talking to the governing board about building a small chapel that can be left open for prayer and shelter. God's house should always be available to those in need, even when no one can be on hand. Don't you think?"

She smiled. "I do, now that you mention it. And what does the board say?"

He lifted his eyebrows. "Mayor Shaw is of the opinion that any fund-raising project ought to wait until after the centennial celebrations conclude."

"Well, that's ten days away."

"So it is." With that, he pushed open the door, revealing the polished wood of a central hall that ran almost the full length of the house. They stepped inside, and he closed the door behind them. The staircase started at the back of the hall, rising above them and making a space for a coat closet next to a door with glass insets. He took her coat and hung it with his in the tiny closet beneath the stairs, stowing her handbag on the shelf above the rod.

"The best thing about this house is the study," he said, indicating the room behind the door with the glass insets. "It has great shelving for my books, and looks out onto the porch so I can always see who's come to call." He gestured to the room opposite.

The wide, open archway required no door. His one Christmas decoration was a somewhat tattered crocheted angel that hung from the apex of the arch.

"It used to belong to my mother," he explained, inviting her into the living room with a wave of his hand.

Though smallish, the living room was cozy and comfortable with the rock fireplace and its impressive, if narrow, hearth. Opening off the living room stood the dining room, and beyond that, the kitchen. Across from the dining room, with a slanted door beneath the narrow staircase, was a bedroom, which opened into the study and a bathroom at the back of the house. Upstairs was a single large bedroom with a roomy closet and a second more modern bath.

"Such a lot of doors," Robin said, coming back down the narrow stairs.

"Mmm-hmm, but it works. They packed a lot of house into a relatively small space, didn't they?"

"They certainly did."

"Let me check our dinner, then I'll show you my second-favorite part of the house," he said, leading her back to the kitchen.

Dinner turned out to be slices of frozen roast beef in gravy, along with baking potatoes and cans of carrots and green beans sitting on the counter. While he checked the entrée, peeling back the foil lid on the disposable tin pan, she looked around. White-painted cabinets and floors gave the room a bright, clean aura, while pale granite countertops and almond-colored appliances kept the space from feeling surgical. She'd have added some fluttery curtains and a few pots of fresh herbs, along with a selection of attractive dish towels and pot holders.

The rest of the house could use some personal touches, too. The living room contained only a nice flat-screen television, a comfortable, if worn, leather chair and a tweed sofa that had seen better days, with a single occasional table between them. The bed downstairs had no headboard. The dresser was rickety, and Ethan used a dining chair as a bedside table and clotheshorse. Her favorite pieces in the house were the antique dining table, china cabinet, which was empty, and chairs. He set the dark cherrywood table with place mats and simple white plates, tan napkins and inexpensive flatware. When she asked, he told her that he'd bought the dining suite and desk from the previous pastor, who'd felt they were too large for his new place in Colorado.

Ethan turned off the oven, opened cans, dumped the contents into bowls and set the bowls into the microwave to heat before herding her into the small mudroom. Leaning down, he hooked a finger in a hole in one of the floor-boards, all of which were painted in the back part of the house, and hoisted it upward. An entire section of floor folded back on hinges, revealing a second narrow staircase. He hit a switch, and a light flickered on below, revealing a room ringed with shelves.

Robin went down in front of him to find herself in a well-lit storage area. Someone had set up a workbench, but she didn't see many tools there now. Instead, Ethan had put in a weight bench and boxing bag. His gloves lay on the workbench.

"Welcome to the Johnson gym," he said. She laughed. "Or the root cellar, as the church ladies call it."

"A root cellar?" Robin parroted. "I don't think so. What great storage, though."

"Next to the study and the bedroom, I spend more time here than anywhere else in the house."

She shot him an amused look. "That's a very 'guy' admission."

"Ahem," he said behind his fist, edging forward. "In case you haven't noticed, I happen to *be* a guy."

She smiled. "I have noticed."

"Yeah? Well, I happened to have noticed that you're *not*."

"Very observant." She giggled.

Above them, the faint ding of the microwave sounded. Ethan rubbed his forehead, murmuring, "Dinner, such as it is, is served." He grabbed her hand and towed her toward the stairs and then up them.

They worked quickly, side by side, to get the food on the table. Ethan had slices right out of the bag for bread, but Robin didn't mind. The meal sat before them on folded towels to protect the surface of the table, and Robin smiled to think that under any other circumstances she might have found the simple, mundane fare unappetizing, but here with Ethan, her hand in his as they bowed for prayer, she didn't want to be anywhere else in the world. No menu, however exotic or sumptuous, could have tempted her away from his side at that moment.

Once before, he'd planned a Sunday dinner for them, and she'd ruined it from fear of the truth. All through the meal, as he served her, playing host with genial ease, she imagined what it would be like to live here in this funny little house with Ethan. As he wielded his knife and fork, chatting and laughing, distracting her from the difficult chore ahead, she began to truly understand what she would really be giving up by leaving here, by leaving him. While eating, drinking, watching her in eloquent silence or holding her attention with teasing banter, he effectively tore out her heart, for none of this would ever be hers. Even if he should come to care for her in the same way that she had come to care for him, what she was about to do would almost assuredly be the end of any hope for them.

If Rusty was right, Jackson had stolen the time capsule, taken the gold, returned the historical papers and the container and let others be blamed for the crime. He had also done all in his power to thwart the repair and reopening of the Beaver Creek Bridge for decades now for no other reason than Shaw family honor; he'd promised his grandfather, who had promised his father, that the bridge would remain closed. Jackson was heir to the people who had killed the bells that hung in the belfry across the street because they'd been donated by an old friend turned enemy. The kind of stubbornness that had made Lucy fake her own death and stay away for nearly ninety long years did not leave a lot of room for forgiveness and acceptance. Jackson had wielded his power as mayor for decades, riding roughshod over anyone who bucked his policies. Why would he tolerate a woman who proclaimed the basic tenet of his family history to be a lie?

If they could keep it within the family, she might have a chance to coexist. Even if Jackson didn't believe her, he might leave her alone so long as no one else knew about her claims, but she couldn't trust Rusty to keep what he knew to himself indefinitely. Once her story became public, people would naturally take sides. Some would not believe her, but some would, and *that* Jackson could not abide. All her dealings with him in the past told her that. What she feared most was that Ethan would come out on her side, and Jackson would go after him in an attempt to discredit her.

Only the intervention of God Himself could prevent such a disaster.

And why should He bother? Robin knew in her heart of hearts that she did not possess the purity of Mary, the mother of Jesus, or the faith of Joseph. All she had at the moment were doubts and fears for Ethan. She no longer cared what the Shaws might say or do to her. She only cared what might happen to Ethan. He deserved success in his first pastorate. He deserved happiness. He loved Jasper Gulch. This had become his home, and he should be able to stay here and enjoy all the respect and support that were his due.

She had seen firsthand today what sort of pastor he could be, how powerfully he could bring the word of God alive for the people, how greatly they respected him for it. How could she possibly let anyone damage that?

Rusty assumed that Lucy would want Robin to have her share of the gold, but Lucy had spoken only of family to Robin. Plus, Lucy had given up everything for the man she loved. She had protected him in the only way she knew how. Robin could do no less.

As they cleared up the dinner leftovers and stacked the dishes in the dishwasher, Robin pondered the situation and wondered if she was making a mistake by telling the

Shaws the truth. She'd been so moved by Ethan's sermon, so challenged by his courage, that she'd acted impulsively, and now she was having second thoughts.

"They've lived all this time believing Lucy was dead, and they'd never have an opportunity to know her now, so what harm is there in letting them go on believing that she died that day in 1926?" Robin asked.

"It isn't the truth."

"The bridge is going to reopen anyway!" she argued.

"And what of Rusty, sweetheart?"

"He's kept her secret this long," she insisted. "Let him take it to his grave."

"He was protecting Lucy," Ethan pointed out softly. "She no longer needs his protection. It's unfair to ask him to carry that lie any further. And what of you? Are you to live with the lie, as well?"

"If I must," she said, lifting her chin.

"Please don't be bound by your fear for me."

She gulped and looked away. "What kind of person would I be if I didn't consider the ramifications of my actions on my friends?"

"Robin, you don't know what Jackson Shaw will do."

"I know what he's capable of."

"We're all capable of great foolishness and even evil, Robin," Ethan pointed out. "Otherwise, the redemptive action of the cross would not have been necessary. I myself have suffered great failures, of which you know nothing."

"You're not responsible for your father's actions, Ethan."

"That's not the point. The point is, Jackson may surprise you. I've seen it before."

"How can I take the chance?"

"Just try to have a little faith. God has a way of working things out for our best, even bad things."

"Still," she argued, "if we can prevent the bad in the first place, isn't that best?"

"Perhaps so," he admitted, "but sometimes we must endure the bad to get to the good."

"I can't risk your future on *perhaps* and *sometimes!*" she exclaimed.

"Robin," Ethan said sternly, "my future is not in your hands."

Well, that was putting it starkly. She had never really believed that she and Ethan would wind up together, that she could truly have him. All along she was always going to wind up back in New Mexico working for the Templeton Foundation for Scientific Research at some cobbled-together job dreamed up by her snobbish but well-meaning parents. Someday they'd present an unobjectionable fellow to her, and she'd be too tired of being alone and too uncaring to resist and so find herself married to him, drifting along with whatever he and her parents wanted. But at least she'd know that she'd done the best thing for a truly good man.

"I'm sure you're right," she answered stiffly, wondering if it was possible to shatter from disappointment. She'd all but decided not to meet with the Shaws, but she made a show of checking the time anyway. "I'd best be going."

Turning, she marched blindly into the hallway. Ethan followed, right on her heels.

"Going to see the Shaws, I presume?"

"That's my business," she told him smartly, arriving at the coat closet.

As soon as she pulled the door open, he reached past her and took her coat from the hanger. "I think I should go with you."

Pretending unconcern, she slipped her arms into the sleeves of her coat and let him tug it up onto her shoulders before reaching for her handbag.

"That's not necessary." She tossed him a smile, keeping her eyelids lowered so he wouldn't see the glisten of her gathering tears. "Thanks for the meal. I enjoyed seeing your house."

"You're welcome," he retorted sharply. "Come again any time."

She nodded, gulped and marched for the door. He stopped her just as she turned the lovely crystal knob.

"If you don't tell them, Robin, I will."

Horrified, she whirled to face him. "Why? Why would you do that?"

Certainty seemed to wash over him, wiping away the anger. He slid his hands into the pockets of his pants. "Because of the collar I wear. Because the Shaws deserve the truth. But it's more than that. This whole town has lived under the bondage of a series of lies for nearly a century. It's impacted their finances, their relationships, access to the town, their safety, even the bells in the church!" He stabbed a finger at the building across the street. "But most of all, for you. This has to end, Robin. You have to be free of it."

He was right, she realized. The truth had to come out, one way or another. So be it. As long as it didn't reflect on him. Nodding, she stepped out onto the porch and turned to face him.

"Fine," she said, "I'll tell them everything."

"Good," he replied, following her to the door. "I'll be praying for you."

She would need his prayers. Oh, how she would need his prayers, and not just about the Shaws. Somehow she had to find the strength to survive leaving this place and this man, for that was what it would come down to in the end.

That was always how it was going to be, no matter that it broke her heart.

Chapter Twelve

Robin could barely think as she drove through town and out toward the Shaw ranch. She was already grieving the outcome. She knew as well as she knew her own name that her only option after this would be to leave town. She only hoped that Jackson would allow her to stay long enough for her to fulfill her commitments to Ethan. She doubted that she would be able to remain past Christmas Day, however. Her job would very likely end within the next hour.

When the lavish log ranch house with the neat metal roof came into view, a strange calm settled over her. The Shaws had chosen the perfect backdrop for their sprawling two-story home. The cloud-dappled blue of the sky and the snowcapped peaks of the evergreen ridges of the mountains reflected in the frozen mirror of the small lake between the great house and the grouping of dusky-red outbuildings. A winding driveway led to a broad archway decorated with a large, impressive statue of a horse rendered in open metalwork. Everything about the place bespoke money and power, but it also had an aura of peace and home about it.

Robin pulled up in front of the tall, handsomely carved door at not quite half past two. She folded her hands over the top of the steering wheel and said a quick prayer for strength, the right words and favor, ending with, "And please, Lord, whatever happens, don't let this rebound badly on Ethan. He's done nothing but good here and doesn't deserve to suffer for my poor judgment."

When she opened her eyes and looked around, she saw that Julie Shaw Travers had come out to greet her. Julie had traded her Sunday best for jeans, boots and a royal blue ribbed turtleneck. She'd caught her long, auburn hair in a loose froth of curls beneath her left ear. At least Robin didn't feel underdressed in her long, A-line, brown wool skirt and matching corduroy jacket worn with a black blouse, black hose and black boots. She opened the car door and got out. Slipping off her coat, she left it in her seat, along with her handbag. She left her keys in the ignition in anticipation of a quick getaway.

"Is the car okay here?" she asked Julie.

"Sure."

Closing the car door, she quickly followed Julie into the house.

The entry hall had been built to impress, with a flagstone floor and a ceiling that soared two stories and showed off a broad, curving staircase that seemed to float in space. Julie waved for her to follow. Sucking in a deep breath, Robin dried her suddenly slick palms on her skirt and rounded a hammered-copper pot the size of a small bathtub filled with poinsettias.

The room that she entered was enormous. The first thing she saw was the Christmas tree. Eighteen feet tall if it was an inch, it twinkled with colored lights. Though many of the decorations appeared expensive, most were of the same homey variety that Mamie had used at the inn, and the effect, while stunning, was also somehow…endearing.

Lush cowhide rugs covered the flagstone floor, and colorful cushions littered the deep hearth of the massive stone fireplace, where a cheery fire blazed. Bulky, overstuffed leather furniture scattered across the large, airy, pine-paneled room. Various members of the family lounged about, talking, reading or watching football on the big-screen television that hung above the mantel, which dripped with holly and ivy that weaved in and around poinsettias, pinecones and candles. A beautiful crèche carved from horn occupied a long narrow table set against one wall. Christmas had come to the Shaw ranch—Christmas and truth.

Nadine and her daughter-in-law, Katie, came into the room at the same time Robin did. Katie carried a tray of steaming mugs.

"Oh, Robin," Nadine said. "Sit down there and have a cup of cider."

Robin sank onto the end of the nearest sofa, but her stomach rebelled at the very thought of swallowing anything. "No, thank you. I'm still stuffed from dinner."

Katie placed the tray on a low, rectangular table and went to scoot into the oversize easy chair next to her husband, her legs draped over his, while Nadine passed a mug to Jackson, who glanced away from the television screen to nod at Robin. The sound on the TV was muted, so Cord and Adam immediately turned their attention to the newcomer.

"Hey, Robin," Adam said, flipping a hand at her.

Julie's husband, Ryan, a popular bull rider, smiled absently at Robin, holding out his hand to his wife, who went immediately to his side, perching on the arm of the sofa near him. Robin had heard that he'd foregone any opportunity to compete in the National Rodeo Finals this year in order to get their ranch established, and she had to admire him for that.

"Where's Faith?" Nadine asked, glancing around the room.

"We're here." Heads turned to find Faith and Dale

Massey leaning over the railing of the upstairs landing. She waved. "Hi, Robin."

Robin couldn't help smiling despite her nervousness. Faith and Dale looked so happy. And why shouldn't they be? In four days they would be married. "Hi."

"Where's Austin?" Faith wanted to know, turning toward the staircase.

"Sent him out for firewood," Jackson said, targeting Robin with his stare. Leaning forward, he took a remote-control device from the table next to the tray of drinks and pointed it at the television, switching it off. Then he set his mug on the table, sat back and crossed one booted ankle over a jeaned knee. While he regarded her, other members of the family helped themselves to mugs of cider, and Faith and Dale descended the stairs. "You have our attention, Miss Frazier," he said, "or do you require Austin's presence, as well?"

Robin gulped. She'd planned a dozen different strategies for this, and only now did she decide how best to proceed. Pulling a simple paper copy of an old sepia photograph from the pocket of her jacket, she unfolded it and rose, passing it not to Jackson but to Cord. She'd been carrying around that old photo for weeks and weeks.

"Do you remember the day we came across the original of this?"

He looked at the photo and nodded. "I do, yes. I still can't get over how much you look like our great-great-grandmother Elaine."

"Elaine," Robin said, "is my middle name. My great-grandmother insisted on it."

"Elaine is my middle name, too," Faith spoke up.

Robin turned to look at her, nodding. "Yes. We're both named after our great-great-grandmother." No one spoke. She glanced around at them before saying carefully, "Elaine Shaw was my great-great-grandmother, too."

"So that's why..." Cord began, looking once more at the picture.

"But how could that be?" Julie asked. "Dad's the only direct descendant of Ezra Shaw."

Jackson shook his head, shifting forward in his seat once more. "Won't do, Miss Frazier. My grandfather was Ezra's only living progeny, and my father was his only living heir, so you cannot possibly—"

"Lucy Shaw was my great-grandmother," Robin interrupted, taking the bull by the horns.

The room fell utterly silent for the space of about five seconds. Then Jackson chuckled.

"That's preposterous."

Suddenly, everyone was talking at once.

"She died going off the bridge."

"The bridge has been closed ever since because of the accident."

"Ezra never got over her death."

"Stole his Model T, didn't she?"

"They didn't ever find a body," someone pointed out.

Jackson shot to his feet, bringing the room to silence again. His expression thunderous, he shook a finger in Robin's face. "That. Is. Preposterous!"

Trembling, Robin backed up a step, but she didn't back down. "Lucy didn't die that day. She staged her death so she wouldn't have to marry Victor Fitzhugh."

Scoffing, Jackson brought his hands to his hips. "Don't be ridiculous. Fitzhugh was a wealthy man."

"Much, much older than her."

"Older men married young girls all the time back then."

"Ezra tried to force her to marry Fitzhugh to save the bank after Silas Massey looted it," Robin stated pugnaciously.

Nadine gasped, and the others traded looks. Jackson just looked thunderous.

"How do you know about that?"

"My great-grandmother told me part of it," Robin divulged carefully. "The rest I've put together since coming here."

Jackson's expression turned ugly. "You scheming, conniving, lying, vicious little—"

"Jackson!" Nadine barked.

He broke off but insisted, "It's obvious she's used her position here to dig up information to use against us!"

"How am I using this against you?" Robin demanded. "My great-grandmother asked me on her deathbed to come here and make myself known to you. I have very little family back home in New Mexico, where she and Great-Grandpa Cyrus raised a daughter, who had two sons, one of them my father. Great-Grandma thought you'd welcome me. But she was very old, one hundred and three, and my parents thought she was hallucinating the whole tale. I had to be sure her stories were true before I approached you."

"And what convinced you?" Jackson asked snidely.

"Well, it wasn't your money and consequence," Robin snapped, folding her arms. "Ever hear of the Templeton Foundation for Scientific Research, Mr. Mayor?"

Jackson frowned.

Dale said, "It's a very well-endowed research foundation established by Jay Ralph Templeton, who made his fortune in mining."

"Jay Ralph Templeton was my great-grandfather on my mother's side," Robin informed them all. "My father and Lucy's grandson, Gary Frazier, is the CEO of the foundation."

"Says you," Jackson retorted.

"It's easily enough proved," Robin pointed out. "Go ahead. Have me investigated. You'll find that Gary Lyle Frazier and Sheila Carol Templeton, both of the Templeton science foundation, are my parents."

"Well, bully for you," Jackson sneered. "So your father married up."

"He happens to be your family, too," she pointed out, insulted.

"You can't possibly prove that."

"Maybe not at this moment," she said, "but I'm not the only one who knows Lucy didn't die that day. Rusty Zidek knows. He's always known. He was there."

"Rusty!" Julie yelped.

"Ask him, if you don't believe me," Robin urged.

"You can't trust that old man," Jackson asserted, punctuating the air with his hands. "Rusty is the next thing to senile."

"Dad, you know that's not true!" Julie insisted.

"I've got nothing against the old man," Jackson said, "but he's ninety-six. She probably planted *memories* in his head that never existed!"

Her voice trembling with anger now, Robin rounded on Jackson Shaw. "Whether you believe it or not, Mr. Mayor, Lucy Shaw faked her death so she could run away with my great-grandfather, Cyrus Gillette. They had a daughter, Dorothy Elaine, who married Lyle Frazier. Together they had two sons, Richard, a college professor who has never married, and my father, Gary, who married Sheila Templeton. Gary and Sheila had me." She thumped herself in the chest. "Just me. So before her death, Great-Grandma Lucy, whom I knew as Lillian, sent me to you, and I came hoping to find family. Instead, I find just what my Templeton family warned me I would find— jumped-up cowpokes and country bumpkins clinging to their consequence too tightly even to share a bit of welcome for one of their own!"

"My own are what matter most to me!" Jackson shouted.

"Really?" Robin sneered. "More than the Shaw-Massey gold? Evidence says otherwise! Well, cling to your gold,

Mayor. I don't want it, I don't need it. And I don't need *you*."

At the word *gold,* Nadine gasped again, and Jackson looked as if he would explode. Now he stabbed a finger at the entry hall, bawling, "Get out of my house!"

"With pleasure," Robin returned sweetly. Then she shook her finger at him. "But don't think you're driving me out of town until I've done what I've promised to do here."

Jackson's mouth dropped open. "What kind of man do you think—"

"The kind who will ride roughshod over anyone to get what he wants! Well, you're not God Almighty, Mr. Jackson Shaw, no matter what you might think!" Suddenly dissolving in tears, she ran from the house.

Behind her, the room erupted with words.

"Is it possible Lucy didn't die?"

"What's this about Shaw-Massey gold?"

"You can't deny that she looks like Elaine Shaw."

"I'm going to talk to Rusty."

"Just be quiet, all of you!" Jackson roared as Robin pulled open the door.

Austin stood there in a shearling coat, his arms full of cordwood. "Robin," he said, smiling. "Mom said you'd be dropping by. Thanks. I was beginning to think I was going to have to stand out here all night waiting for someone to let me in. How are you?"

She ran past him without a word. Obviously confused, he trailed her with those blue eyes so like her own, turning on his heel as she skirted the bumper of her car, yanked open the driver's door and dived behind the steering wheel. She was sobbing openly by the time she got the engine started.

All the way back to town, she meant to drive straight to the inn. She imagined calling her parents and telling them just how right they were about the Shaws then promising to return to New Mexico to start her new job with the foundation after the first of the year. The way Jackson had sneered at her parents had infuriated her. He knew nothing of them, and yet he had automatically assumed they were beneath him. And to think that she had scolded her mother for her snobbery toward the Shaws! Her parents would be elated to know that the Shaws had rejected her just as they'd predicted, and that she was coming home to take the job they'd created for her. Part of her couldn't help feeling defeated and disappointed, but after the hateful rejection she'd just received, it would feel good to be wanted. Besides, she'd known for some time how this thing would play out. She'd reconciled herself to it beforehand—except somehow she hadn't, which was why instead of driving to the inn, she drove straight to the church instead, not even to the parsonage, where she'd left Ethan earlier, but to the church, because something told her that was where he would be.

She slung her coat over her shoulders, locked her handbag in the car and hurried up the walk, stowing the keys in a pocket. The door opened easily at her touch. She found Ethan laying out a length of artificial evergreen garland, which he obviously meant to drape from the belfry, as the trap was open and the ladder was down.

"Should've locked that," he said with a smiling sort of grimace. "Wouldn't want anyone to see the ropes on the bells, but I just couldn't resist the urge to slip over here and enjoy the view for a while. Thought I'd do a bit of decorating while I was at it."

She started to sob, still clasping her coat together. He opened his arms, and she threw herself across the room, straight into them.

"I should have gone with you," he said against her hair.

She shook her head again. "No. I had to do this on my own. But just as I knew they would, they *hate* me."

"Give it a little time, sweetheart. You've had, what? A year and a half to get used to the idea? They've only just learned that the family history they've known all their lives is a fiction."

"Jackson was livid."

"Yes, I imagine he was," Ethan said. "Wouldn't you be if you were in his shoes, er, boots?"

She honestly hadn't thought of it that way. Wiping her eyes with her hands, she pulled back to consider. "Yes, I suppose so."

"What did he say exactly?"

"Oh, he said the whole idea of Lucy surviving the accident on the bridge was preposterous and that I'd used my position here to dig up details to make my story believable."

Frowning, Ethan said, "I suppose we should've foreseen that. Did he fire you?"

Shocked, she realized that he hadn't. "No, actually, he didn't. Not yet anyway."

"Well, that's something. What else did he say?"

"He accused me of planting memories in Rusty's mind."

"Now, *that's* preposterous," Ethan retorted.

"And he called me scheming, conniving, lying and vicious."

Ethan's face hardened, and he said, "That was uncalled for. I really should have gone with you."

She shook her head. "It wouldn't have made any difference. Might even have been worse."

"What about the others?" Ethan asked, his brow furrowed. "Did no one believe you?"

Shrugging, she admitted, "I'm not sure. They had questions, certainly, but Jackson is the one I have to convince. You know that."

"He'll think it through," Ethan assured her, "and he'll come around."

"You say that now, but you don't know what Jackson may do. Maybe I should just leave town before he has a chance to act."

"You will not," Ethan insisted, "I need you here. How would I get through Christmas without you?"

Of course, Christmas. Even in her anger, she'd made it clear to the Shaws that she planned to remain in Jasper Gulch until after the holiday. She managed a nod.

"I'll stay then, my Christmas gift to you."

"That's all I want for Christmas," he told her, kissing her in the center of her forehead.

That might be all he wanted, but he deserved so much more! He, too, had family who refused to acknowledge him, family who should be here with him, supporting him, celebrating this holy holiday with him, loving and appreciating him. Robin had let herself be distracted from contacting his sister before, but that wouldn't happen again.

"Come on," she said, sniffing. "I'll help you hang the garland before I go." Perhaps her time here was short, but she meant to enjoy every moment of it.

"Great," he said, catching one end of the greenery.

He headed to the wrought iron ladder, climbing it up through the trapdoor in the ceiling. She slipped on her coat, draped the other end of the garland around her shoulders and followed him up. Hammer in hand, he tacked up a nail on the outside of the belfry and looped the greenery around it before moving carefully to the next corner to repeat the process. Robin fed him the garland in measured lengths, making sure that he got the drape right and that the greenery was hung securely at each juncture. When they came to the end of the garland, they were left with only two short, very narrow wires with which to attach it.

"You hold it in place while I tie the wires together," Ethan said, going down on his knees on the narrow ledge around the inside of the belfry.

Robin mimicked his pose, going down on her knees beside him. He reached around her with one arm so he could use both hands to get the tiny wires fastened.

"There," he said. "I think that's got it."

As she fluffed and straightened the garland, he kept his arm about her. She looked up to find that he was gazing off across the housetops and the valley floor to the mountains beyond as if transfixed. She couldn't blame him. Even from this perspective, the view stunned the eye. It somehow seemed fitting that they should take it in on their knees.

Robin could not resist the urge to lay her head on Ethan's shoulder. He put his cheek against her crown. They said not a word for a long while, but eventually the cold became too much to bear.

"We should go below," Ethan urged softly.

Nodding, she let him help her to her feet, then followed him down the ladder. He closed the trapdoor and stowed the pole.

"I have to leave," she said. "I need to make some phone calls. I have to speak to Rusty, for one, warn him that I told Jackson what he knows."

Nodding, Ethan agreed. "He won't mind. He was prepared to tell the story himself, if you recall."

"Still, I can't let him be blindsided by Jackson in a fury, if it's not already too late."

"You're right. You're right."

Wrinkling her nose, she muttered, "I lost my temper and mouthed off about the gold."

Ethan let out a long, low whistle. "And how did that go over?"

"Nadine couldn't have been more horrified. The others were clearly mystified, and that's more or less when Jackson threw me out."

"Hmm, well, I suspect we won't have long to wait before we know what happens next. Will I see you tonight at the evening service?" he asked.

She made a face. "I don't want to run into any of the Shaws just yet. Will you let me know if you hear anything?"

"Sure. How about lunch tomorrow?"

She shook her head. "I don't know if I'll even get a chance to grab a sandwich while working. There's so much to do. Dinner tomorrow night?"

"Wedding practice and rehearsal dinner."

"Oh, right."

"I could meet you about six-thirty at Great Gulch Grub for breakfast the next morning," he offered tentatively.

She shook her head. "I don't think you ought to be seen in public with me."

He threw up his hands. "I'll bring it to the inn, then."

She smiled and gave him two thumbs-up. "Deal."

"You are one stubborn woman."

"Just concerned," she refuted, heading for the door.

She hurried out, already reaching into her pocket for her keys and cell phone. Rusty would be her first call, but at some point she intended to speak to someone in California.

She'd do whatever it took to reunite Ethan and his sister. She might never be part of Ethan's family, but she would do everything in her power to give him back what family he already had.

Maybe that was the point of it all. Maybe that had been God's plan all along. Maybe, just maybe, He had brought her here, not to claim her own family, but to help Ethan reunite with his.

If so, she would count the cost worth it and go home glad, even if she had to leave a big chunk of her heart behind here in Jasper Gulch, Montana.

Chapter Thirteen

Ethan had expected Jackson to be skeptical, even angry, but to accuse Robin of using her position at the museum to dig up material with which to essentially blackmail the family went far beyond acceptable to Ethan's way of thinking. And to call sweet Robin scheming, conniving, lying and vicious! Well, Ethan hadn't been prepared for the white-hot rage he'd felt when she'd reported Jackson's words to him.

Only the need to soothe her emotionally distraught state had kept his anger in check until she'd left. Still, not immediately confronting Jackson Shaw about his treatment of Robin was probably a good thing. Cooler heads would surely prevail by the time of the evening service.

As expected, Robin did not put in an appearance, and the only Shaws to show up at the service were Cord, Austin and Faith. Katie, Cord's wife, left as soon as the service ended. Austin, Cord, Faith and Dale stayed behind, lingering until everyone else had gone. Ethan girded himself for a showdown, for if they didn't bring up the meeting with Robin, he would. Austin broached the subject without fanfare.

"You know about Robin's claim?"

"I believe it's more than a claim. I believe it's fact."

"The story's just so crazy," Faith said. "Our whole lives we've believed that Lucy died when Ezra's Model T went off the bridge."

"That's what you were *supposed* to believe," Ethan pointed out.

"If Robin just hadn't waited so long to come forward," Dale said, "I think it would be easier for everyone to accept."

"I understand that," Ethan told him, feeling some relief that they weren't rejecting Robin's assertions out of hand, "but her own parents cast doubt on the story, and you have to understand how much Robin loved her great-grandmother. She didn't want that dear lady branded a liar or a lunatic. Robin felt that she needed proof before she came forward. Then she got caught up in the centennial celebrations, and there was the disappearance of the time capsule and its contents. No sooner did she find the proof she needed—"

"That photo of Great-Great-Grandmother Elaine," Cord put in.

"Exactly. She hadn't even decided what to do with that when Dale showed up, then with everything she and Olivia had uncovered about Silas Massey looting the bank, well, she didn't know what to do. When Dale and Faith became engaged, Robin began to fear that if she came forward, you'd all think she was opportunistic."

Dale and Faith exchanged glances, but Cord said, "Because of the Massey money, you mean, but that doesn't quite track. Not if she's a granddaughter of the Templetons."

"Which you must know by now she is," Ethan said, folding his arms. "But you're conveniently omitting any mention of the gold."

"There's no proof this Shaw-Massey gold even exists!" Cord exclaimed.

"Are you sure about that?" Ethan asked. "Maybe you'd better talk to Rusty Zidek before you make up your minds."

"That's exactly what we're going to do," Austin said.

"Meanwhile," Ethan warned, "you tell your father to behave himself where Robin Frazier is concerned. He's skeptical. I understand that. But she does not deserve name-calling—"

"We're sorry about that," Faith put in quickly. "I'm sure it was just the shock of the whole thing."

"Or threats," Ethan went on.

"No threats were made," Dale assured him.

"But it would help if we could keep a lid on this," Cord added, "for the time being, at least. Just until we figure out what's what."

Ethan nodded, satisfied. "I think Robin feels the same way."

"I, for one, just don't understand what she hopes to gain," Austin said. "I wasn't there when all this went down, so I only know what the others have told me, but if she's not after money, then what's the point?"

"All she's ever wanted is family," Ethan told them. "Don't you get it? All she's after is the connection, just to be part of something bigger than herself. You all have that. You're Shaws. You have brothers and sisters and now sisters-in-law and brothers-in-law. There will be nieces and nephews soon, cousins, grandchildren to fill your parents' home. For Robin, there's just Robin. As it stands now, her children will have just each other, and who's to say they won't fall out? Who will they have then?

"Robin's great-grandmother was her anchor," Ethan went on. "She was family going back three generations, but that's all gone now. Lucy must have seen it on her death-bed. She must have realized that she had cheated Robin of the extended family that she so desperately needs, and she tried to give it back to her. She tried to give *you* to

Robin, and I have to say that Robin deserves better than you've given her so far."

Faith, for one, looked abashed and sorrowful, and Dale, at least, seemed to understand.

"I can identify with that," he said. "We Masseys have family all over the place, but we don't have what the Shaws have, and I didn't even realize it until I came to Jasper Gulch." He kneaded Faith's shoulders and kissed the auburn crown of her head, saying, "It's part of why I fell in love with you."

"Poor Robin," she whispered.

"I don't think she's entirely alone," Cord said, giving Ethan a half smile.

"She's not," Ethan stated forthrightly, "and don't think I'll let anyone drive her away."

"Dad said you had bottom and wouldn't be easily moved," Austin told Ethan with an approving nod, "and from him that's high praise."

"Well, I appreciate that, Austin," Ethan said, "but can you guarantee that he won't go after her? We all know he could drive her out of town if that's what he's determined to do."

Austin traded looks with his sister, who said, "Dad can be a hard man when it comes to family, and for Dad it always comes down to family. But he's not by nature vicious or unfair."

Ethan bowed his head. That wasn't quite the reassurance for which he'd hoped.

"Look," Ethan said, "I respect Jackson, but I *believe* Robin."

"But then," Dale ventured softly, "you're in love with her. Right?"

Ethan didn't deny it. He couldn't. So he said nothing at all.

"We'll see you tomorrow as planned," Faith said, sounding apologetic.

"Wedding rehearsal," Ethan acknowledged stiffly. "I, uh, believe you have a recording for me."

"Oh, yes. I almost forgot." She took the tiny thumb drive from her pocket and passed it to him. "Just so you know about how long each selection will be."

After clearing his throat, he asked, "No vocals?"

Because Faith played the violin for the symphony orchestra in Bozeman, the Shaws had arranged for a string quartet from there to provide music for the wedding, but they wouldn't arrive until Christmas afternoon.

"Sadly, no," Faith replied. "It's difficult to arrange these things for Christmas Day. Fortunately, my friends in the orchestra were willing to oblige me. Otherwise, we'd have to make do with recorded music only."

"I'm sure it will be lovely," Ethan told her.

The Shaw brothers had gone, and Faith and Dale were almost out the door when Dale suddenly turned back, calling out, "Oh, Pastor!" He came hurrying back to Ethan, extracting an envelope from his coat pocket as he did so. "Faith's not the only one to almost forget something important. I wanted to pass this along to you tonight, for services *about to be* rendered."

He handed over the envelope, which was quite surprisingly thick. "Dale, I have the feeling this is too much," Ethan said, but Massey shook his head.

"No, I sat down and tried to figure out what it's worth to me to be married to Faith by a man whom I both like and respect here in this town and church that my family helped found, and the price is, quite frankly, incalculable. Besides, I can afford it. Plus, I have the feeling you could use some extra cash right now." He leaned close, adding, "And FYI, I did a little research, and I have it on good authority that there's an excellent jeweler in Bozeman." He gave Ethan the name before hurrying back to Faith.

Ethan slid the envelope into his pocket with a grateful nod. He tried to take comfort in this unexpected largesse and Dale's even more unexpected information, but he couldn't help wondering what it meant. Was this God telling him that he had reason to hope? But how could he when he was still hiding secrets? Ugly secrets that no woman could be expected to forgive.

Rusty could not have been less concerned about Jackson Shaw or more pleased that Robin had finally revealed Lucy's secret. He cackled with glee over the whole thing, but Robin could not feel so sanguine about it all. The confrontation with the Shaws had gone pretty much as she'd expected, and yet she felt bone-deep disappointment that left her with a fragility she hated. That being the case, she took the coward's way and decided not to call her parents. That didn't keep Robin's parents from calling her, however.

After she talked to Rusty, she returned to her room at the inn and succumbed to the luxury of a hot soak in the tub to try to calm her frayed nerves before phoning California. When the bedside phone first rang, she groaned and considered not answering, certain whom she would find on the other end of the line. Ultimately, though, she yielded to the dictates of honoring one's parents.

Her mother made a very good argument that Robin needed to "put some mental distance" between herself and Jasper Gulch by visiting her Templeton grandparents' Santa Fe home for a while. Afterward, her father took the phone to say that they would miss her if she stayed away for the holiday.

"I really have obligations here that I can't get out of." Robin refused apologetically, praying they wouldn't ask her about the Shaws.

"One of them wouldn't be named Ethan Johnson, would it?" her father wanted to know.

Robin pressed the mole beneath her eyebrow, sure they'd finally come to the point of this parental double-teaming. "He's the pastor here."

"And the nephew of Molly Johnson and the brother of Colleen Connaught."

Oh, she should have seen that coming.

"That's true," she conceded, a sense of inevitability settling over her. "What about it?"

"Do you know that his father is in prison for manslaughter?"

"I do, yes, but that doesn't have anything to do with Ethan."

"Well, the gang shooting that killed one Theresa Valens certainly has to do with him."

"Gang shooting," Robin parroted, her head spinning. "Ethan wouldn't be involved in any gang."

"Are you sure about that?" Gary asked.

"Y-yes," she stammered. "Did you miss the part where I said he is a pastor here?"

"Doesn't sound like pastor material to me."

"Well, I assure you he is," Robin stated briskly, her mind awhirl. "Now, I have to go."

She didn't remember hanging up the phone or toweling off and changing into her pajamas. She just kept hearing Ethan say that he'd made mistakes about which she knew nothing, that he had his own secrets. She remembered his sermon about Herod killing the Jewish boys in an attempt to murder the predicted Jewish king and how Ethan had drawn a correlation between that and the gang killings in his old neighborhood in L.A. So much that he'd said and she had dismissed suddenly took on new meaning.

We all have secrets... I intend to reveal all of mine, just gradually.

What do you propose to do? Live with the lie? I can tell you from experience that it isn't easy to do.

I myself have suffered great failures of which you know nothing.

Some might disapprove...

He'd been especially concerned that her parents would disapprove of him, and now she had to wonder exactly why. Because of his father? Or because he, Ethan, had been in a gang?

She'd heard that it was impossible to leave a gang once you were part of one. Could Ethan be hiding out in Jasper Gulch?

No, no, that made no sense. He wouldn't be hiding under his own name. Besides, Ethan was a true pastor; anyone could tell that.

Still, it hurt to think that Ethan hadn't told her about this, hadn't explained. All the while he'd been pressing her to tell him *her* secrets, he'd been holding back his own.

That frightened her. The truth must be ugly, indeed, for Ethan to behave like this, and she couldn't help feeling that she was owed the truth.

Perhaps it would make leaving him and Jasper Gulch easier, but it didn't feel that way. Instead, she felt robbed, cheated. And not by Jackson Shaw.

Robin did not greet Ethan with a smile the next morning. He assumed that it had to do with her confrontation with the Shaws the afternoon before, so he wasted no time telling her about his conversation with Cord, Faith, Austin and Dale after the evening service. To his surprise, she seemed barely to listen, watching in silence as he laid out the foil-lined cardboard containers with their breakfast inside as he spoke. Afterward, she mentioned that her parents had called to try to convince her to come home to

New Mexico for Christmas. His heart pounding, he asked if her plans had changed.

"That depends," she said, staring at the scrambled eggs and ham he'd just uncovered.

"On what?" he asked carefully.

She looked up, spearing him with her round, blue gaze. "On what happened to Theresa Valens."

Theresa. The bottom dropped out of Ethan's stomach. So his past had finally come to call. He didn't know why he was surprised. Strange, he hadn't expected it to play out quite this way.

"Your parents had me investigated, I guess."

"Does that matter?"

"I suppose not."

"I need to know what happened to her, Ethan."

"Of course you do. I've meant to tell you all along."

"Tell me now."

He sat down at the little table with her and waited, letting her lead. She didn't hesitate.

"Who was Theresa?"

"My girlfriend."

"I see." Robin thought for a moment and asked, "How old were you?"

"Seventeen. She was sixteen. We were just kids and sure we were in love the way only kids can be."

He could tell Robin was disturbed, but she sat silently and finally asked, "How…how was she killed?"

Swallowing, he pushed the words past a hard knot in his throat. "We went to the same school, had the same friends pretty much, except her brother was in a gang, and I wasn't."

"You weren't in a gang?" Robin asked, her gaze sharp.

"No." She seemed to relax a bit. He hated to tell her the rest. Nevertheless, he went on. "But my best friend was."

"The same gang as her brother?"

A rather astute question. "No, and that was the problem. I tried to stay neutral."

"Sounds dangerous," she commented, frowning.

"You know what they say about teenagers," he responded gruffly, "especially teenage males. They think they're invincible. Bad stuff only happens to the other guy."

"Except that isn't true," Robin pointed out.

"No," he agreed. "That isn't true. Oh, it worked for a while, but one night there was a fight, three against one. My buddy told me to stay out of it, but one of them had a knife. He went for my friend from behind. All I did was step up and lift my arms to block the attack, but that didn't matter to the other gang. It didn't even matter that I got cut." He unbuttoned his cuff and rolled back his sleeve to show the long, jagged scar. "Or that my buddy was beat up real bad and put in the hospital. I had stood up to them, and that made me the enemy."

"Oh, no," Robin whispered, closing her eyes.

"After that, everything went crazy," he recalled. "Theresa's brother forbade her to see me again and put out a hit on me. Meanwhile, my friend's guys were out looking for anybody connected with the beat down. The cops were talking about a gang war. I thought Theresa and I should just blow town and let them have at it. I actually thought I could take her to Ireland to my mom's folks or something equally stupid like that."

"What happened?"

"I had her meet me in what was supposed to be neutral territory. And within a minute she was dead on the curb beside me. They were gunning for me, but they got her."

"Oh, Ethan, I'm so sorry."

"She wasn't the only one I got killed," he gritted out. "Her brother and four other people died before the cops got a handle on the situation."

"It wasn't your fault!" Robin exclaimed.

"Wasn't it? I thought I could walk the line, live in no man's land, break all the rules. I was Johnny Jack Johnson's boy, tough by association. A young fool!" he scoffed. "So six people died in a gang war."

"All you did was love a girl and try to help a friend," Robin argued.

"Yeah. Worked out really well for everybody, didn't it? Oh, I know gang life means dying young. That's why I tried to stay out of it. But if I'd stayed away from Theresa, she'd still be alive today."

"You don't know that. You just said that gang life means dying young. It sounds to me as though her brother was the one who put her in danger, and you, too."

"You sound like Pastor Rick," he said softly, almost smiling again.

"Who's Pastor Rick?"

"Pastor Rick is the reason I'm here," Ethan told her. "He got me off the streets and back into school. He's the reason I got into church and pulled it together. He helped me find God. Because of him, I know what real love is. Together we got my buddy out of that life."

"That's wonderful!"

"Yeah, it is," Ethan admitted.

After a moment, she asked, "Are you ever afraid that the gang will catch up with you?"

He shook his head. "No. There's hardly anyone left. Those gangs were small, and they don't exist anymore. Their members all left the life or died on the streets or in prison."

She reached across the empty space between them and took his hand. "I'm glad you didn't get involved in gang life, but I'm sorry for all you've been through."

"What I've been through has made me who I am," Ethan said. "The former pastor here wasn't so sure how the congregation would react to the truth about my past, though, so he advised me to say nothing until I felt I was well established in Jasper Gulch. I've wanted to speak up, but with all this centennial craziness going on, it's hard to know just how folks will react."

"I see what you mean," she told him. "I've been wondering if I'm ever going to know Jasper Gulch at normal. But, Ethan, no one can blame you for Theresa's death."

"Thank you for saying that," he told her, beyond grateful for her reaction. "But I was as much to blame as anyone."

"No. You were kids, little more than children."

"Children playing grown-up games," he pointed out.

"But look what you've done with your life since!"

He wanted to hug her for that. Her opinion was not, however, terribly realistic. "I wonder if your parents would agree with you about this."

She opened her mouth to argue, but then she closed it again, averting her gaze.

"I didn't think so," he said softly, his heart aching.

"Maybe I don't care if they approve or not," Robin suddenly cried, lurching up from the table and whirling away.

Ethan's heart turned over inside his chest, an oddly bittersweet happiness filling him. She wouldn't say that if she didn't care a great deal for him. Rising, he went to her and turned her into his arms.

"You must care what your parents think," he told her gently. "God commands us to care. But He also promises to help us. Hear the Word of God from the book of Isaiah— 'Fear not, for I am with you, be not dismayed, for I am your God, I will strengthen you, I will help you, I will uphold you with My righteous right hand.' We have nothing to fear from the truth now, sweet Robin, nothing. You have laid your truth before the Shaws, and I have laid mine before you. After Christmas, I will lay mine before the church. The outcome belongs entirely to the Lord, but you should know that from this moment forward, I will be asking Him for you. Do you understand what I'm telling you?"

"Yes, Ethan," she said calmly, sliding her arms about his neck. "I understand."

He kissed her ear. "Good. Now eat your breakfast."

Keeping his arm around her, he walked her to the table and seated her.

They'd said no words of love, made no promises and they had no guarantees. No one knew yet what Jackson Shaw would do, and Ethan wouldn't, couldn't, go against her parents. The church could very well dismiss him when they heard about his past. Still, he and Robin had made a commitment of sorts. They had shown each other their hearts, and he would beg God day and night for his heart's desire in this matter until she was either his or the door was forever closed on the possibility.

Meanwhile, they had Christmas, Christmas in Montana. That in itself was something for which to be thankful.

He drove to Bozeman after breakfast, feeling that a weight had been lifted from his shoulders. Nadine had requested that Ethan wear white ecclesiastical robes for the wedding ceremony, robes he did not possess. He had to borrow them from a pastor in Bozeman. At least, he told himself, his secrets were now all exposed, and Robin had borne them with more love and equanimity than he'd had any right to expect. He could only hope that the church would feel the same and that her parents would somehow reconcile themselves to a prospective son-in-law from the wrong side of the tracks, for he suddenly could not see his life without Robin anymore.

On pure impulse, Ethan decided to visit the jeweler recommended by Dale Massey before heading back home. It was more than impulse really, more like a driving urge that Ethan felt compelled to obey. He told himself that it was the height of foolishness, that he was just going to look, that no good could come from even window-shopping. Then, of course, he found the perfect ring, a ring that might have been made for Robin's finger.

Ethan dithered for an hour, recounting for himself all the reasons why he would be reckless, indeed, to get his hopes up. Robin's parents were not likely ever to approve of him. Regardless of what Jackson Shaw did, Ethan could very well find himself without a pastorate or any other living, not to mention a place *to* live. Another thing weighed on his mind: Robin wanted family above all else, and he was the last man able to give her that, considering that what family he had wouldn't even speak to him. Still, that ring fairly shouted at him.

The jeweler was patient and helpful, though he admitted that praying over an engagement ring was a first for him. Nevertheless, he tolerated Ethan's indecision with equanimity. In the end, Ethan simply could not leave without that ring. He decided that the purchase was an expression of hope, and he silently vowed to carry it on his person until such time as he could use it or was forced to return it.

He spent the remainder of the day in prayer, rising from his knees in his church office only at the last moment to prepare for the wedding rehearsal.

The details seemed endless. Robin spent the day with Olivia, preparing exhibits, stocking the gift shop, which would be staffed by volunteers yet to be trained, and going over plans for the grand opening. How they would manage to get everything done Robin couldn't imagine, but she was grateful for the distraction. At least she didn't have time to dwell on her fears, which had taken on new significance at breakfast.

Ethan had as good as declared that he loved her, but he wouldn't marry her unless her parents approved, not that it mattered. She couldn't possibly marry him so long as Jackson was a threat to him, and this new information about Ethan's past would just give Jackson more ammunition with which to drive him away. Robin dared not let it come to that. Her only recourse now was to leave town before she got Ethan into trouble. She was prepared even to deny her great-grandmother's claims, if necessary, and she'd make sure that Jackson knew it. Before she left, however, she would give Ethan what Jackson Shaw would deny her: family.

More determined than ever, she drove home after work, fell on her knees and emptied her heart to God. She asked for nothing for herself. Compared to Ethan, she'd had a fairy-tale existence. Perhaps her parents wouldn't agree, but she knew Ethan, and he deserved every happiness that she could give him.

With that in mind, Robin dried her face and found the number that had the local exchange for Valinda. That was most likely the landline. Huffing out a breath, she dialed the number and waited. A no-nonsense voice came on the line after the first ring.

"This is Colleen."

Filled with both euphoria and terror, Robin began to speak, the words tumbling out of her mouth with unaccustomed speed.

"Colleen, my name is Robin Frazier. You don't know me, but I'm a friend of your brother's, and I want to give you to him for Christmas. Please, just hear me out."

It was tough going for a bit. Colleen did not seem receptive at first, but she didn't hang up. Soon, Colleen was asking for details about her brother's life. Before Robin knew it, an hour had passed, then two. By the time the call ended, Robin felt that God had answered at least one of her prayers that night, and she went to bed praising Him.

Chapter Fourteen

When the Shaws arrived that evening, Ethan stood awaiting them, quite resplendent, he thought, in shiny black patent-leather shoes, black slacks, white collar and shirt, full-length white robe and knee-length dark red stole embroidered with white doves.

Nadine pronounced him "Wonderful!" and went on to worry about the reception at the Shaw ranch that would follow the wedding. "I pray it doesn't snow!"

"Everything will be fine, Mom," Faith assured her. "If it snows, we'll get out the sleighs. The neighbors have already said we can borrow from them."

"That's true, and what a pretty ride that would be from the house to the barn."

As soon as everyone arrived, Ethan got them all into place and queued up the music. The Masseys were there en masse, including Dale's mother, Ronna, as well as numerous townsfolk. Ethan couldn't help noticing, however, that Jackson seemed unusually quiet, tense and haggard. So be it. Let the mayor stew in his own juices for a while. No one said a word about Robin, Lucy or Rusty Zidek, and Ethan was content to let the matter rest. This was Faith and Dale's time. The focus should be on them.

He walked the wedding party through their traditional

roles, making adjustments as they requested, until all knew their parts. Then it was time to make the trek out to the Shaw ranch for the rehearsal dinner. This, too, would be good practice, as it would tell them how much time it would take for a group to begin gathering at the ranch after the wedding. He noted that the caterer from Bozeman was on hand to time the event right down to the second.

They had an excellent barbecue-chicken buffet waiting for them at the Shaw house. Ethan managed a chat with one of Dale's younger brothers, his best man. He watched Dale expertly referee a sarcastic duel between his divorced parents, and breathed a sigh of relief when Nadine swept Ronna off to the barn to look over the preparations for the reception.

A Shaw barn was undoubtedly nicer than the homes of many people, and situated as this picturesque red behemoth was beside the beautiful blue bowl of a small lake, Ethan felt it would do nicely as the site of the wedding reception. The whole county would likely be in attendance, and Ethan had heard that the Shaws had rented furniture for the lofts so people could relax and talk in comfort. Still, a barn was a barn to some folks, and he wondered how Ronna Massey, being a wealthy New Yorker, would view the event. She hadn't seemed to think much of their little country church.

Logs. How quaint.

She hadn't seemed impressed with the town, either.

Jasper Gulch seems less a place than a name with pretensions.

Dale had smiled at Faith in apology more than once throughout the evening. Faith, for her part, didn't seem to mind Ronna's snootiness. As crazy as it seemed, Ethan understood that. He knew that he'd welcome Sheila Templeton Frazier's snobbery, if only she and her husband would welcome him into their family.

His heart felt heavy inside his chest as he drove back to the parsonage later. The funny old house had always felt homey and cozy until he walked through the door that night. Suddenly, the place felt empty and hollow. He wanted to find Robin there waiting for him, wanted to see her curled up on the sofa in the living room, reading or watching TV, wanted her smile of welcome and acceptance.

He got himself ready for bed, carrying the little velvet-covered box everywhere he went. He sat down in the dark on the side of the bed, placed his cell phone and the ring in its box on the seat of the chair that served as bedside table and bowed his head. He began to pray, confessing his inadequacies as well as his dreams, begging for guidance, for surety, for signs. He asked God to bless Robin, to give her the joy and the family that she deserved. He prayed for her parents, that they would open their hearts fully to the man God chose for her, even if that was not him.

He went on to pray for the Shaws and the Masseys, for Faith and Dale in particular, and soon he was naming just about everyone in the town—the McGuires, Mamie, the Middletons, the Franklins, the Harcourts, the Lakeys, Wilbur down at the bank and Myrtle at the diner, the Masons, Rusty, Coach Randolph and Deputy Sheriff Calloway, the Shoemakers and Coopers, Abigail, Chauncey, the women in the a cappella quartet, even Pete Daniels, wherever he'd gotten off to—and then the town itself.

He literally emptied his heart of every concern for his town, his church and the woman he loved. Then he began to pray for his family. He prayed for his father, that his faith would hold true through his incarceration and especially afterward. He prayed for his aunt, who had been like a mother to him in so many ways. He prayed for his little niece, who had never known her own father. He prayed for his sister's broken, unforgiving heart.

When he had wrung himself dry like an old rag, he slipped beneath the covers and blanked his mind for sleep, weary to the pit of his soul. As soon as he began to drift away, his phone rang.

He didn't think about not answering or even look at the caller ID. At this time of night, the call would be important, and it was a pastor's lot in life to share the bad news that often came to his congregants at a late hour. He swiped a thumb across the bottom of the screen even as he lifted it to his face.

"This is Pastor Ethan."

"Well, now," said one of the dearest voices on the planet, "then this would be Pastor Ethan's sister, calling to wish him a merry Christmas."

Every time the phone rang the next day, Robin expected to hear Ethan's voice telling her he'd heard from his sister. She did not expect to hear Rusty Zidek's.

"Just thought you'd wanna know that the Shaw boys came to see me."

"Oh? And did they believe you?"

"Hard to say," Rusty admitted. "I think they wanted to, but it seems to all come down to the gold. Without proof that it exists, they can't quite swallow the rest."

"And we have no proof that the gold exists," Robin said around a sigh.

"To prove it exists, we'd have to prove Jackson took it," Rusty told her.

That was it, then, Robin thought. They were beat.

It began to snow late in the afternoon. Ethan finally called—to ask if Robin could come early for quartet practice. Assuming that the other ladies had expressed concern about being on the roads after dark with the snow coming down, she asked Olivia if she could take off early.

Olivia shrugged and laughed. "Go on. Your mind's been somewhere else all day anyway."

Robin couldn't help feeling depressed. Between Rusty's news and wondering why Colleen hadn't called, she didn't feel terribly upbeat. It didn't help, either, that she and Olivia were working on a display of antique wedding dresses, including a beautifully beaded Arapaho garment on loan and Elaine Shaw's simple cotton tulle frock, now aged to the color of tea. Robin kept imagining her own wedding dress, one she doubted she'd ever get to wear.

A particular dress from the late fifties had especially caught Robin's eye. With a simple straight skirt and long sleeves, it seemed terribly elegant, especially as it was topped by a little hooded cape trimmed in feathers. Robin thought that style would be lovely for a winter wedding, especially if the feathers could be replaced with high-quality faux fur. She might even cut off the skirt at tea length and add fur to the hem, not that it mattered. She wasn't going to marry in winter, not in Montana anyway. She almost wished she didn't have to see Ethan again, and drove over to the church only reluctantly to find Ethan alone in the vestibule.

"Once again, I am in your debt," he said, his eyes shining as he caught her hands with his.

Relief and joy suffused her. "Colleen called you."

"We talked late into the night. It was so good to hear from her. I cannot thank you enough."

"I'm just glad it worked out." At least something had.

Ethan reached into the pocket of his jeans and drew out a tiny, velvet-covered box that made the breath seize in Robin's throat. "Glad enough to marry me?" he asked, placing the box in her upturned palm.

As she opened the hinged lid with trembling fingers, he explained that he'd phoned her father that morning.

"We had a long talk. He didn't say that he approved of

our marriage, but he did say that he only wanted your happiness. I'm convinced that with a little time we can win his full blessing."

"Oh, Ethan," Robin gasped, her eyes swimming with tears. "It's so beautiful." She blinked so she could keep the delicate ring with its sizable diamond in sight for a moment longer. Then she closed the lid on the little box and pressed it back into his hand, her heart breaking. "But I can't."

"Robin." He made it half plea, half scold. "I can't believe I've misread you in this."

"I spoke to Rusty earlier," she told him tonelessly. "It's over, Ethan. We can't fight Jackson."

"I don't accept that."

"Nevertheless, I'll be leaving right after Christmas."

The other ladies began arriving then. Even as she quietly dried her eyes, she was perversely glad. She couldn't resist the sanctuary of Ethan's arms, no matter how temporary, and that would only make leaving more difficult. At least she would take with her the knowledge that he and his sister had made peace. She would know that he'd loved her enough to ask her to marry him, and that she hadn't cost him his pastorate and his home.

She didn't know how she managed to sing after that. Her throat felt thick and clogged, and the backs of her eyes burned with unshed tears. Ethan seemed positively morose and lethargic to the point almost of paralysis. He didn't even go into the sanctuary to play the bells from there.

To Robin's surprise, Faith dropped by during the practice with last-minute questions for Ethan about her own wedding. Her first comments, however, were words of praise for the music.

"I've never heard anything so lovely! Could you possibly sing this song for my wedding Christmas night? I mean, since you're all invited to the wedding anyway."

"But we're not all invited to the wedding," Robin blurted.

"Of course you are," Faith said, taking her hand. "I know it's short notice, but it would be a simple thing to slip out here just before we say our vows, sing and slip back inside again, and the song is perfect. Don't you think so, Ethan?"

"We might leave out the bells to make it less Christmassy," he said, staring at Robin.

"I wouldn't want to upset your father," Robin muttered to Faith, who waved that away.

"Oh, don't worry about him," she said, leaning close. "He's got Dale's mother for that now. It's fine. Trust me." She squeezed Robin's hand. "Please."

Robin made a face. "You're very kind to ask after the way I insulted your family. I shouldn't have said those things. You and your brothers and sister have never been anything but polite to me."

"You were provoked," Faith said. "We all understand that. Now, will you do me the honor of singing at my wedding?"

"Of course," Robin acquiesced. She hadn't meant to leave on Christmas Day anyway. Besides, it would give her a chance to speak to Jackson, to tell him that she was leaving and would deny her great-grandmother's claims, if necessary.

Faith hugged her. "Thank you! Oh, I'm so thrilled. I'll make sure the musicians know about the change. Now, if I could have just another moment of your time, Ethan…"

He walked off with her, and they conversed for several moments. He nodded, and Faith rushed out. The other ladies began to gush about being asked to sing at Faith Shaw's wedding. Robin only hoped Jackson wouldn't make a scene, but why would he? That would just make her claims public, and surely he wanted to avoid that.

Before she left for the evening, Ethan tried to convince

her to talk to him, but she knew that would only make what she had to do that much more difficult.

"Robin Elaine Frazier," he scolded her, "where is your faith?" Then he reminded her that he would see her the next afternoon.

For the first time, she regretted agreeing to help him with the Christmas program, but she'd given her word, and she only had two more days to get through.

Then it was just a matter of getting through the rest of her life without him.

Ethan had chosen the hour of five o'clock for the Christmas Eve service for several reasons. It allowed the congregation to enjoy the pageant and still get home in time to spend the evening with their families. Also, given the unpredictability of winter weather, it seemed wise to have everyone off the roads as early as possible. Finally, and most important personally, five o'clock came an hour before the regularly scheduled recorded carillon of the bells, which meant that his bells could not be confused with those. Ethan had decided to toll each bell every minute for ten minutes, *bong-bong,* then to ring them continuously for a full minute, hoping they would play themselves out for several moments afterward.

He promised the cast and crew of the pageant a surprise, then warned them not to abandon their posts before hurrying out to remove the shelves for the last time, Robin at his side, both dressed in period clothing.

"I can get someone else to help me if you want," he offered morosely, but she shook her head.

Grudgingly relieved, Ethan prepared to ring the first bell at a quarter to five. It wouldn't have been the same without Robin. They'd been in this together from the beginning, and he wouldn't have wanted to do this without her. He didn't want to do anything without her, and he resented her refusal to marry him, even if she did it to protect him. Didn't she have any faith at all? Didn't she see that God had worked out every problem so far? Surely all they had to do was give Him time to work out the rest.

The first peal reverberated throughout the building and across the countryside just as the sun sank below the western peaks, followed quickly by the deeper bong of the larger bell. The effect was startling, lyrical. Through the open doors of the sanctuary, they could hear people asking what that was. When the second toll began a couple seconds later, they heard applause. With the third came shouts of praise.

Robin kept time for him with a stopwatch. He pulled the ropes, one after the other, with several seconds of silence between each lovely *bong-bong.* People poured into the church from outside, the Shaws among them. They crowded the vestibule, gathering around the closet to watch him pull the ropes. When he began the arduous eleventh minute, Brody Harcourt and Ellis Cooper stepped in to take over. His arms and chest burning, Ethan gladly yielded. Both were grinning and gasping for breath when Ethan brought the exercise to a stop sixty seconds later.

People stood around looking upward with their hands in the air, marveling at the sound and feel of the bells as they continued to toll. Robin hurried into the sanctuary ahead of Ethan, no doubt to avoid the Shaws as much as to get the cast and crew back into position. He took his place, promising to explain about the bells. He did so as soon as the congregation and the bells quieted.

"The bells were a gift to the church from Silas Massey and his wife, Grace," Ethan explained. "They fell into disuse after the Masseys left Jasper Gulch, but they are obviously sound, so Robin and I acquired new ropes, attached them to the bells and planned to surprise you all by ringing them today to call you to this Christmas Eve

service. It seems fitting as this is our centennial year." He
looked pointedly at Jackson Shaw then, asking, "Don't
you agree, Mayor?"

Jackson stood, nodded and said, "I do, indeed, Pastor,
very fitting."

Ethan felt a pang of regret that Robin's great-grandmother's
wishes for her were not to be fulfilled, but then he mentally
scolded himself for a lack of faith, the same lack of faith that
he'd been telling himself Robin had displayed by rejecting his
proposal. How was she to have faith if he could not?

Ethan prayed aloud, put on his smock over his period
clothing, and the pageant began. The bells had set the tone
for the production, which went with as few hitches as possible when children and animals were involved. Poignant
in places, precious in others, it somehow managed to be a
reverent retelling of the Christmas story, and the timing
couldn't have been better as the congregation filed out just
as the preprogrammed recorded carillon played "Silent
Night" through the speakers in the belfry.

The cast seemed jubilant afterward, even as they hurried away, with Ethan's blessing, to join their families for
their personal Christmas Eve celebrations. A few stayed
behind to help clear the sanctuary of the pageant set and
prepare it for the Christmas-morning service. To his disappointment, Robin was not among them. She'd slipped
away before he could speak to her. Perhaps, he decided, it
was just as well. He didn't know what he might say or do
in his current state of mind. He only knew that he loved
Robin and that she wouldn't marry him out of some mis-
guided attempt to protect him from Jackson Shaw.

Well, who was going to protect Jackson if the mayor
went after Robin, who had never meant harm to anyone
in her life? God Almighty surely would not let that pass.
Ethan himself would not let that pass, pastor or no.

After the sanctuary was restored to its normal state,

Ethan locked up, changed his clothes, then walked across the street to the parsonage. To his surprise, he found a package on the front porch, addressed not to him but to Robin, though the address was clearly that of the parsonage. It even said, "C/o Parsonage, Mountainview Church of the Savior." The return address was a street in Albuquerque, New Mexico. *Overnight* had been stamped all over the thing.

Blessing the parcel-delivery service, Ethan loaded the thing, which had considerable heft, into his car and drove it straight to the inn. He knew that Robin had been invited to join Mamie and several of her guests for a Christmas Eve celebration. He knew this because he had been invited, too. That being the case, instead of going to Robin's room, he went to the great room of the lobby.

The old-fashioned tree there had been up for so long and had dropped so many needles that it was beginning to look a tad spindly. In fact, many of the decorations on Main and Massey streets were looking worse for the wear, as some had been up for six weeks or more now. The fresh snowfall lent it all a clean, sparkling quality, however.

Mamie greeted him with a mug of hot apple cider in her hand. "Glad to see you. Maybe you can cheer up our girl."

"I don't know about that," he said, shouldering the heavy box. "Maybe this will, though."

He carried the box over to the chair near the rock fireplace where Mamie led him.

Robin looked up, frowning, to ask, "Ethan, what have you done?"

Bending to place the box at her feet, he shook his head. "Not me, sweetheart. You refused my gift, if you recall. Your parents had this overnighted to the parsonage. At least I assume it was your parents."

Ignoring his reference to the engagement ring, she studied the box. "That's their address."

He produced a pocketknife so she could cut through the packaging. Two minutes later, she caught her breath, looking at the jumble of pieces encased in bubble wrap.

"It's Great-Grandma's antique brass floor lamp." Abruptly, she dropped her face into her hands and began to cry.

Ethan looked at Mamie, who seemed as puzzled as he was. After several seconds of Mamie's ineffectual patting, Ethan did the only thing he knew to do. He simply scooped Robin into his arms.

"It's all right now," he told her, holding her close. "There's no reason to cry. I'm sure your parents thought you'd like the lamp."

"I love the lamp!" she wailed against his shoulder. "Don't you see? It was always meant to be mine when I m-m-married! All of Great-Grandma's antiques are."

He glanced at Mamie, wondering how much she knew. Apparently she knew enough, for she bustled away, herding the others in the room toward the kitchen by promising them treats.

"You haven't told your parents that you turned me down," he guessed gently.

Robin shook her head. "I haven't even told them that you asked, but they must have assumed...and this is their way of giving us their blessing."

He closed his eyes, whispering, "Thank You, God." One more hurdle cleared. One more problem solved. If a man couldn't believe in that, what could he believe in?

Shifting onto one knee, he dug the tiny ring box from his pocket. "Robin Frazier," he said, "I'm not just asking you to promise to marry me. I'm asking you to perform an act of faith. Put this ring on your finger as a sign that you believe God will make a way for us."

She took the box, but she didn't open it. Instead, she hedged. "What if Jackson—"

"Jackson Shaw is not God, and he's made no move against either of us."

"But—"

"Robin, sweetheart, once the church learns about my past, they may not want me anyway."

"Of course they will!" she insisted. "You're a wonderful pastor, and you love it here."

"I love *you*," he told her. "Just put on the ring, Robin, and instead of waiting to see what Jackson will do, wait to see what God will do."

She stared at him for a long moment. Then she opened the box, took out the ring and slid it onto her finger.

He let out a silent breath of relief, kissed her and said, "Merry Christmas, my love."

She melted onto his shoulder, sighed and asked, "Have you ever considered taking a pastorate in Albuquerque?"

He laughed, but at the same time he was praying.

Oh, Lord, we're depending on You, all of us, me, Robin, the Shaws, the church, even this town. This can end well, with truth and forgiveness all around, or it can go the way so much of human history has gone, with half measures, hidden motives, resentments, broken relationships. If it's Your will that I leave here under a cloud, I'll leave here under a cloud, and I'll trust You to bring me into the sunshine again somehow, but it seems to me that this town and this church have lived under a cloud long enough. I'm asking You to make it right, for Your own glory in this, the season of glory.

Meanwhile, Ethan planned to take joy in all that he could. The pageant had gone well, and the bells had been restored to the church. Robin's parents had given their blessing for her marriage to him, and in time they might even be pleased about it. Ethan and his sister had made their peace. Robin had Ethan's ring on her finger, and he could hope and pray that his faith would be vindicated.

True, Jackson hadn't accepted Robin as part of the family, so her great-grandmother's hopes had not been realized, but the bridge would reopen at last, thanks to Dale Massey. The museum would open, too, and the new time capsule would be buried. The gold remained missing, but so be it.

The long centennial celebration would at last come to an end, and Jasper Gulch would begin life with a new normal. Ethan hoped that he and Robin would be part of that for a long time to come, but what mattered most was that they live out God's will for them, hopefully together.

Please, Lord, he prayed, *wherever and however You say, but please let it be together.*

Chapter Fifteen

They rang the bells on Christmas morning, Robin and Ethan working in tandem. Even the Masseys showed up for the 10:00 a.m. service, which was well attended, meaningful and joyous. The a cappella women's quartet quietly assumed their positions in the foyer as Ethan opened the service with a prayer, then took up the handbells secreted beneath the pulpit and began to toll the beat for the song. When the women's voices rang out, rich and sweet, people literally gasped. Afterward, the ladies received rousing applause. The singers slipped into the sanctuary between short Bible readings and joined in carols accompanied by the piano and a pair of guitars. Finally, Ethan recited a poem, then closed the service with a blessing.

To Robin's delight, he had spoken to his sister again that morning, as well as to his niece, Erin, and his aunt Molly. "So this has already been the merriest Christmas I've had in years," he'd said, hugging her.

To hear people say that they had been pleasantly surprised twice, first with the bells and then with the a cappella quartet, made Robin smile. Ethan obviously felt a great sense of accomplishment, and she was delighted to have been a part of it. Having his ring on her finger made everything that much sweeter, though she knew it might ultimately cost him.

They'd made no announcement, but she saw people glancing at her hand and heard murmurs of speculation. Apparently so had the Shaws, because Nadine and Jackson made a beeline for them as soon as the service ended.

Feeling Ethan's protective arm slide about her waist, Robin braced herself for a confrontation. She hadn't told Ethan that she planned to deny her great-grandmother's claims; she feared he would object and ruin everything. Before either of them were put to the test, however, Deputy Sheriff Cal Calloway appeared at Jackson's shoulder, speaking quietly into his ear. Jackson nodded, spoke to Nadine, and the pair turned away, following Calloway from the building.

"That's odd," Robin murmured.

"You never know what God's doing, sweetheart," Ethan told her as Olivia and Jack McGuire bore down upon them. After that, they had time only for hugs, congratulations, best wishes, "I told you so!" and "Merry Christmas!"

Lacking a formal dining space at the inn, Mamie had offered to make Christmas dinner at the parsonage. Ethan and Robin had eagerly taken her up on the offer, even when she'd asked to invite several others to join them: Rusty Zidek, Abigail Rose, Chauncey Hardman and a couple from the inn, all folks who would be alone for the day. Robin had never eaten venison roast for Christmas, but then she'd never before spent Christmas in Jasper Gulch, Montana.

After the jolly but somehow tense meal, which took a long time to prepare and clean up, Robin hurried off to the inn to dress for Faith's wedding. She met the other members of the women's quartet in the vestibule to practice one last time, without the handbells, before the wedding, then went off to find Ethan.

He was in his office, putting on his robe.

"Wow," she said, smiling. "Never thought I'd like a guy in a skirt, but you look very handsome, and there's a certain authority in that robe."

Ethan laughed. "You look great, much too fine for this humble preacher."

She'd chosen the royal blue dress that he liked so well and paired it with a lacy shawl. The sides and front of her hair she'd twisted into a loose, elaborate knot atop her head, leaving the back to flow in a sleek fall past her shoulders. She wore a bit of eyeliner tonight, along with a stroke of mascara and a dab of red lip gloss, which she'd had to replace after she kissed Ethan, with some thoroughness and just a hint of desperation, before returning to the other members of the quartet.

They all sat together in a pew at the back of the church to await the beginning of the ceremony. Marie Middleton, lovely in a fluttery dress, came to tell them when they were to slip out and sing, then hurried off to attend some other detail.

Austin and Adam Shaw, dressed in black Western-style tuxedos with red rosebuds in their lapels like their brother Cord, lit the many candles in the church, which was beautifully decorated with its centennial Christmas finery and pew bows of gold-and-silver netting tied about long-stemmed red roses. The Massey men all wore gray tuxedos, with red rosebuds in their lapels.

Jackson wore the same black tuxedo as his sons when he escorted Faith down the aisle. She looked gorgeous in a white satin strapless bodice with a long-sleeved chiffon overlay and full gossamer skirt. Being petite, she was short enough to pile her lovely auburn hair on top of her head and set her long billowing veil in place with a coronet of white roses to match those in her bouquet.

The ceremony went off without a hitch. Afterward,

Ethan rang the bells in joyous cacophony while the guests left for the reception and the wedding party gathered for photographs. Ethan and Robin had agreed that she would wait for him in the parsonage, but to her surprise, Jackson called out to her before she could leave the sanctuary.

"Robin, would you mind hanging around? I have something I need to say."

Suddenly fearful, she sat down again. Was she going to have to publicly recant? Would Ethan even allow it?

After only a few photos, Jackson dismissed the photographer, as well as Marie, then he deftly got rid of the Masseys, asking Dale's brothers to head out to the ranch to oversee the parking situation and make sure everyone was safely and conveniently being transported down to the barn where the reception was to be held. He assigned Dale's father the task of stand-in host and even went so far as to ask Ronna Massey to check on the caterer and make sure all was running smoothly on that end until he and Nadine got there.

Ethan had removed his robe to ring the bells. Now he draped it over a pew and came to sit beside Robin, looping his arm about her shoulders protectively. When the room had been cleared of all but family, Ethan and Robin, Jackson walked to the center of the aisle right in front of the altar and put his hands together, obviously gathering his thoughts. Finally, he spoke.

"Guess there's no way to say this except to come right out with it. I am a thief."

Nadine shot to his side. Some present laughed, thinking it a jest. Some gasped.

Ethan looked at Robin, clasped her hand and whispered, "Thank God. I knew He wouldn't let Jackson live with this for much longer."

Robin bit her lip, tears welling in her eyes. If only she'd

had such faith! Then again… She looked at the ring on her finger and smiled.

Nadine quelled the outburst with sharp gestures of her hands. "Now, now. Let Jackson explain. He has his reasons."

Jackson glanced at Robin, saying, "I don't know how she knew, but Robin was right. There is gold. It was hidden in the time capsule."

"So that's why Pete Daniels took it!" Cord exclaimed.

Jackson shook his head. "Pete tried to steal the time capsule, just to cause trouble, I expect, but I caught him digging it up. Then I got rid of him and opened it myself out of sheer curiosity. I didn't know about the gold until I saw it and read the accompanying note. It was meant for all Shaw and Massey heirs to share equally."

"Oh, Dad," Faith said, clinging to her brand-new husband.

Jackson nodded, looking at Dale. "I'm sorry, Dale. That was before we knew you. At the time, all I could think was that the Masseys are rich in their own right and they got that way on money stolen out of the bank that our two families started here in Jasper Gulch, money my family had to struggle for years to cover for our investors and depositors. It just didn't seem right that your family should then turn around and recoup the gold in the time capsule. So I took matters into my own hands."

"I can understand your motivation," Dale said, "knowing what Silas did." Faith tightened her arm around his waist.

"But what about all the vandalism and the notes?" Cord asked.

"That's where I made my worst mistake," Jackson admitted, clapping a hand to the back of his neck. "Pete figured something was up when I didn't turn him in but let everyone think the time capsule had been stolen. If I'd just taken the gold and let everyone find the rest, I might have gotten away with it, but there wasn't time for that. I panicked and hid the whole thing. Pete tried to force my hand by vandalizing things around town and sending those cryptic notes to throw suspicion onto Lilibeth Shoemaker."

"Now, there's where you're wrong," said a familiar voice. Rusty Zidek pushed into the sanctuary from the foyer, letting the door swing closed behind him. Obviously, he'd stayed behind to listen. "I sent those notes."

"You!"

"That's right. I knew 'bout that gold, see. Just like I told you." He stabbed a finger at Cord.

"But how could you know?" Nadine demanded.

"Lucy Shaw told me," Rusty insisted. "Just like I said. L.S. stands for Lucy Shaw. She told me 'bout that gold long before she faked her death and ran off with Cyrus. And I told Robin when I figured out she didn't know. See, I recognized her right off. Why, she couldn't look more like Elaine Shaw if she was her twin."

Julie walked up to Robin and took her hand. "So you really are Lucy's great-granddaughter."

Robin nodded, tears rolling down her face. "Yes, I am."

Jackson wilted. "I knew she had to be," he said, "but admitting that meant admitting that the gold existed and I was the one who took it, and I was just too ashamed to do it until now." He sucked in a deep breath and went on. "You all should know that Pete Daniels has been seen around town again. Deputy Sheriff Calloway told me today, and I will not have Pete arrested for my crime. I'd hoped to keep him away, but this is as much his home as mine, and I'm as responsible for whatever he's done as he is."

"But you've returned the time capsule and everything publicly owned," Ethan pointed out, looking to Robin.

"That's right," she said, sniffing. "So long as the private

property is dispensed of as it should be, what real crime have you committed?"

Nadine looked around hopefully, the tracks of tears on her face.

"As far as I'm concerned," Dale said, "my family only has to know that they have some money coming. I wish I could say that they'd pass it by when they learn the truth about Silas, but..." He grimaced. "I wouldn't count on it. My share can go to the city of Jasper Gulch, though. That ought to pay for some of the damage."

"That's where mine will go, for sure," Jackson rumbled, sounding choked up. "And whatever else happens, I intend to announce my resignation as mayor tonight."

Nadine slipped her arm through his in a show of support. She'd be standing by her man through thick or thin. He kissed her cheek.

The Shaw sons all traded looks. "Does that mean one of us is going to have to take over as mayor?" Cord asked reluctantly.

"Eh, what's wrong with Ellis Cooper?" Rusty wanted to know.

"Not a thing," Jackson said. "Ellis is a good man, and maybe it's time for the Shaws to step aside and just concentrate on family."

"I'm for that," Cord said, clasping Katie's hand.

Jackson's gaze sought out Robin's then, and he said, "You're part of this family, Robin, though you may wish otherwise now. What do you say?"

She had to clear her throat and blink away the tears. She could barely believe it. Jackson Shaw admitting that she was family, asking for her opinion. Suddenly she realized that her every hope had been fulfilled far beyond her wildest dreams. She looked to Rusty, who smiled, his crinkled eyes gleaming, and gave her a satisfied nod, as if to say his work was now done. Recalling what he'd said about her great-grandmother knowing from heaven what transpired here on earth, she finally managed to croak, "I say, thank God!"

"Then let's do just that," Jackson rumbled. "Pastor, would you lead us in prayer?"

"It's my honor to do so," Ethan said, getting to his feet and bringing a quietly weeping Robin with him. "My very great honor."

Ethan called a meeting of the church council two days after Christmas. Still reeling from Jackson Shaw's resignation as mayor, they listened to Ethan's explanation about his past with ill-concealed impatience, thanked him for his honesty and hurried home to their families.

As Rusty Zidek put it, "Son, we already knew you were no lightweight. Keep up the good work."

Mick McGuire had another take. "There's rich fodder for some mighty fine sermons."

And that, as they say, was that.

The city council decided in very short order that bringing charges against anyone served no purpose, as nothing belonging to the community had been taken and all damages had been covered, with a nice nest egg left over for the city coffers. Ellis stepped into the mayor's shoes gladly and, with Jackson's full blessing, oversaw the ribbon cutting at the bridge on New Year's Eve and the dedication of the museum, which opened to rave reviews. The new time capsule was filled and buried—without any hint of gold or any other valuable being included.

As for Jackson, he declared that his new occupation was to be hassling his children about providing him with grandchildren.

Neither Robin nor Ethan had any desire to prolong their engagement. They decided to marry on New Year's Day, right in the middle of the newly reopened Beaver Creek

Bridge, just about at the spot where Ezra Shaw's Model T had gone into the water on that fateful evening so long ago.

"Who in her right mind would choose to get married out of doors in the middle of winter in Montana?" Sheila Templeton Frazier wanted to know as she helped Mamie fluff the fur on the edge of the satin-lined cape that hung about Robin's shoulders. "Though I have to admit, it's a very pretty dress."

Mamie, God bless her, had called all around Bozeman until she'd found the right dress in the right size and the right fabrics to make the cape, to which she'd added the most beautiful sequined fasteners and appliqués. As Robin dressed for her wedding at the inn, she said a silent goodbye to the little room where she had spent the past six months.

The Shaws had graciously insisted that her parents stay with them at the ranch. They, too, were family, after all, and Sheila and Gary seemed suitably impressed with their quarters. The Shaws and, therefore, Jasper Gulch had risen considerably in their estimation.

The groom would wear his ministerial collar, at Robin's insistence. The pastor who would conduct the ceremony came from L.A. with Ethan's sister, niece and aunt, who had hit it off with their hostess, Mamie, as if they were all old friends. Robin was delighted to meet the famous Pastor Rick, who had come prepared with full ecclesiastical robes for the wedding. Ethan's niece, Erin, would serve as flower girl, though the only flowers were to be the white roses in Robin's bouquet and the petals in Erin's basket.

In deference to the weather, they kept it short and sweet. No music, no poetry, no candle lighting or long processions. Just a couple in love, a minister and their witnesses standing on a bridge beneath a winter sun in the sight of God. Livvie attended as matron of honor, but it pleased Robin that both Julie Shaw Travers and Faith Shaw Massey offered to do so. Jack stood up with Ethan, grinning at his wife the whole time Robin and Ethan repeated their vows.

Pastor Rick had a few surprises up his ecclesiastical sleeve. While Ethan kissed his bride, Rick sent a discreet text message. Suddenly, bells pealed across the valley floor, filling the air with their joyous music.

Those residents of the town who did not brave the cold to stand out on the bridge during the brief ceremony waited back at the church until the happy couple arrived for a cake-and-punch reception. Amidst the gaiety and laughter there, Ethan's cell phone rang.

Robin watched emotion wash over her husband's face as he softly said, "Hello, Dad." Then, "Yes, I wish you could've been here, too. She's a wonderful woman. You'll love her."

Colleen stood nearby, and she looked away, but Pastor Rick quickly positioned himself so he stood directly within her line of sight. Robin knew then that Rick had arranged the call. The burly, middle-aged pastor stepped forward, bent and whispered something into Colleen's ear.

She shook her head and pushed past him, but as she brushed by Ethan, she said, "Wish the old man a happy new year from me."

Ethan's expression contained such joy in that moment that Robin could not resist the impulse to take his hand in hers, as she would so often over the coming years. She recalled then the words that he had quoted to comfort and encourage her when her faith had been weak and lacking.

They were the very words that would be carved above the door of the lovely stone chapel erected on the campus of the Mountainview Church of the Savior, one that never closed: a place for prayer, a shelter in time of storm, a shade in the heat of the day. Built with Robin's share of the Shaw-Massey gold, the chapel would become a popular place for small weddings and other ceremonies. These timeless words from Isaiah 41:10 would be there through the generations to strengthen all who worried and wondered:

"Fear not, for I am with you; be not dismayed, for I am your God; I will strengthen you, I will help you, I will uphold you with my righteous right hand."

So had learned the pastor's wife with her first—but not by any means her last—Montana Christmas.

* * * * *

If you liked this BIG SKY CENTENNIAL *novel,
make sure you read the entire miniseries:*

*Book #1: HER MONTANA COWBOY
by Valerie Hansen
Book #2: HIS MONTANA SWEETHEART
by Ruth Logan Herne
Book #3: HER MONTANA TWINS
by Carolyne Aarsen
Book #4: HIS MONTANA BRIDE
by Brenda Minton
Book #5: HIS MONTANA HOMECOMING
by Jenna Mindel
Book #6: HER MONTANA CHRISTMAS
by Arlene James*

Dear Reader,

While it's true that not all secrets are equal, secrets *can* be poison. They can destroy friendships, marriages, families, entire communities, even governments. Even well-meaning, well-reasoned secrets can become heavy burdens and require substantial "upkeep." What was simply meant to go unsaid may soon have to be covered up, and that means obscuring the truth or telling a lie. One lie begets another and another and… You get the picture.

For a Christian, keeping a secret long-term can have the same effect as an infection in the bloodstream. The longer that secret is there, the worse the "host" feels.

That's what Robin and Ethan each learn as they find their way together. Thankfully, they don't have to deal with it all on their own; thankfully, neither do we. Our Lord can be trusted with our every secret, because He knows it all—and loves us—anyway.

God bless,

Arlene James

Questions for Discussion

1. The Shaw family invested heavily in the community of Jasper Gulch from its official founding, helping to build and support the town, through the church, the bank, the city government and the economy. However, did they have too much influence in the town?

2. Lucy Shaw's staged accident on the Beaver Creek Bridge caused that bridge to be closed for nearly ninety years, shutting off one of only two routes of access into and out of Jasper Gulch. This is an example of a secret that impacted an entire community. Can you think of any secrets that have impacted entire communities or even societies in real life?

3. Robin's parents doubted her great-grandmother's confession. Why would they do that? Can you think of true instances when people confessed to having other identities and faking their own deaths and were doubted?

4. Robin's "proof" for her great-grandmother's confession consisted of the details of the story (some of them not widely known), the corroboration of a witness (Rusty Zidek), her own middle name—which was the same as her supposed great-great-grandmother's—and her amazing likeness to that same great-great-grandmother as seen in an old photograph. Would that be enough for you to make your case? Would it be enough for you to accept her claim? Why or why not?

5. Jackson Shaw knew well that Silas Massey had looted the Jasper Gulch bank in retribution for Ez-

ra's not allowing him to reclaim his share of the gold buried in the time capsule when Silas's investments had gone awry. Because the Shaw family had then struggled for years to cover the bank's losses and keep its depositors and, thereby, the community afloat, Jackson felt justified in taking the gold for himself and his family. Was this reasonable? Why or why not?

6. Robin feared that Jackson would reject her claims and possibly even force her out of town. She knew that the Shaws had managed to keep the bridge closed for decades, had kept secret the looting of the bank by Silas Massey and had "owned" the mayor's office since the city's founding. She had seen Jackson in action. Did her fear seem reasonable? What did her fear say about her faith?

7. Robin's need for family connection drove her great-grandmother to confess her secrets on her deathbed and led Robin to seek the truth in Montana. Some say the need for family connection is a basic human drive. Do you think that is true? If it is true, why do you suppose we have so many broken families?

8. Ethan had his own secrets. We all have pasts, and we all have difficulties, but do we hold pastors to a different standard? Why?

9. The former pastor counseled Ethan not to immediately reveal his past. Instead, he advised Ethan to give himself time to settle in and let others come to know him better before revealing his past. In a real-life situation, have you ever given such counsel?

10. Had Ethan not had his own secret, would he have been so sensitive to and understanding of Robin's situation? Did his family's estrangement make him more sensitive to and understanding of her reason for coming to Jasper Gulch? In general, is it not our shared experiences that make us better friends, more able servants, sincere condolers, wise advisers?

11. Secrets, secrets, secrets! But are all secrets bad? The Shaws kept the looting of the bank a secret so the bank wouldn't fail. This saved depositors from losing their money, but it gave Jackson a motive for stealing the gold in the time capsule. Good or bad?

12. Lucy Shaw faked her own death via an accident on the bridge so she could marry the man of her choice. Robin was the ultimate result, but so was the closing of the bridge. Good or bad?

13. Robin came to Jasper Gulch under the guise of writing a paper on genealogy so she could investigate her great-grandmother's story and possibly find family. Good or bad?

14. Ethan kept quiet about the death of his girlfriend in a gang shooting and his father's incarceration, hiding the depth of his own turnaround in the process. Good or bad?

15. Rusty Zidek kept Lucy's secret for eighty-eight years. Then he went on a secret campaign of sending mysterious notes. Good or bad?

16. In the end, Jackson Shaw saw the error of his ways, confessed all, stepped aside as mayor, made restitution

(and then some) and generally played a part in fulfilling Ethan and Robin's faith. Does this ever happen in real life? Can you share an instance of it?

COMING NEXT MONTH FROM
Love Inspired®

Available December 16, 2014

HER COWBOY HERO
Refuge Ranch • by Carolyne Aarsen
When rodeo cowboy Tanner Fortier ropes ex-fiancée Keira Bannister into fixing his riding saddle, the reunited couple just might have a chance to repair their lost love.

SMALL-TOWN FIREMAN
Gordon Falls • by Allie Pleiter
Karla Kennedy is eager to leave Gordon Falls, but working with hunky fireman Dylan MacDonald on the firehouse anniversary celebration has this city girl rethinking her small-town future.

SECOND CHANCE REUNION
Village of Hope • by Merrillee Whren
After a troubled past, Annie Payton is on the road to recovery. Now she must convince her ex-husband she's worthy of his forgiveness—and a second chance at love.

LAKESIDE REDEMPTION
by Lisa Jordan
Zoe James returns home to Shelby Lake for a fresh start—not romance. So when she starts to fall for ex-cop Caleb Sullivan, will she have the courage to accept a second chance at happily-ever-after?

HEART OF A SOLDIER
Belle Calhoune
Soldier Dylan Hart can't wait to surprise pen-pal Holly Lynch in her hometown. But when he discovers that sweet Holly has kept a big secret from him, can their budding romance survive?

THE RANCHER'S CITY GIRL
Patricia Johns
Cory Stone's determined to build a relationship with his estranged father, but when he invites the ill man to join him at his ranch, Cory never expects to find love with his dad's nurse.

LOOK FOR THESE AND OTHER LOVE INSPIRED BOOKS WHEREVER BOOKS ARE SOLD, INCLUDING MOST BOOKSTORES, SUPERMARKETS, DISCOUNT STORES AND DRUGSTORES.

LICNM1214

REQUEST YOUR FREE BOOKS!

2 FREE INSPIRATIONAL NOVELS
PLUS 2
FREE
MYSTERY GIFTS

Love Inspired

LI13R

Keira wished she could keep her hands from trembling as she handled Tanner's saddle. What was wrong with her?

Seeing him again, his brown eyes edged with sooty lashes and framed by the slash of dark brows, the hard planes of his face emphasized by the stubble shadowing his jaw and cheeks, brought back painful memories Keira thought she had put aside.

He looked the same and yet different. Harder. Leaner. He wore his sandy brown hair longer; it brushed the collar of his shirt, giving him reckless look at odds with the Tanner she had once known.

And loved.

She sucked in a rapid breath as she turned over the saddle on the table. Tanner seemed to fill the cramped shop.

Keep your focus on your work, she reminded herself.

"So? What's the verdict?" Tanner asked.

"I don't know if it's worth fixing this," she said, quietly. "It'll be a lot of work."

Tanner sighed. "But can you fix it?"

"I'd need to take it apart to see. If that's the case, two weeks?".

"That's cutting it close," Tanner said. "Is it possible to get it done quicker?"

Keira would have preferred not to work on it at all. It would mean that Tanner would be around more often.

It had taken her years to relegate Tanner to the shadowy recesses of her mind. She didn't know if she could see him more often and maintain any semblance of the hard-won peace she now experienced. Tanner was too connected to memories she had spent hours in prayer trying to bury.

"I'm gonna need it for the National Finals in Vegas in a couple of weeks." Tanner continued.

"I heard you're still doing mechanic work, as well?" She was pleasantly surprised she could chitchat with Tanner, the man who had once held her heart.

"Yup, except last year I bought out the owner. Now I'm the boss, which means I can take off when I want. I took over the shop in Sheridan after a good rodeo run. The same one I started working on before—" He didn't need to finish. Keira knew exactly what "before" was.

Before that summer when she left Tanner and Saddlebank without allowing him the second chance he so desperately wanted. Before that summer when everything changed.

A heavy silence dropped between them as solid as a wall. Keira turned away, burying the memories deep, where they couldn't taunt her.

But Tanner's very presence teased them to the surface.

She looked up at him to tell him she couldn't work on the saddle, but as she did she felt a jolt of awareness as their eyes met. She tried to tear her gaze away, but it was as if the old bond that had once connected them still bound them to each other.

Will Keira agree to fix Tanner's saddle?
Pick up HER COWBOY HERO to find out.
Available January 2015, wherever
Love Inspired® books and ebooks are sold.

SPECIAL EXCERPT FROM

Love Inspired
SUSPENSE

*SWAT team member Isaac Morrison didn't plan to
fall for his best friend's sister. But when Leah Nichols
and her son are in trouble, he'll stop at nothing to
keep them out of harm's way.*

Read on for a sneak peek of
UNDER THE LAWMAN'S PROTECTION
by Laura Scott

"Stay down. I'm going to go make sure there isn't someone out there."

"Wait!" Leah cried as Isaac was about to open his car
door. "Don't go. Stay here with us."

He was torn between two impossible choices. If someone had shot out the tires on purpose, he couldn't just
wait for that person to come finish them off. Nor did he
want to leave Leah and Ben here alone.

So far he wasn't doing the greatest job of keeping
Hawk's sister and her son safe. If he'd been wearing his
bulletproof gear he would be in better shape to go out to
investigate.

Isaac peered out the window, trying to see if anyone
was out there. Sitting here was making him crazy, so he
decided doing something was better than nothing.

"I'm armed, Leah, so don't worry about me. I promise
I'll do whatever it takes to keep you and Ben safe."

He could tell she wanted to protest, but she bit her lip
and nodded. She pulled her son out of his booster seat

and tucked him next to her so that he was protected on either side. Then she curled her body around him. The fact that she would risk herself to protect Ben gave Isaac a funny feeling in the center of his chest.

Leah's actions were humbling. He hadn't been attracted to a woman in a long time, not since his wife had left him.

But this wasn't the time to ruminate over the past. Isaac's ex-wife and son were gone, and nothing in the world would bring them back. So Isaac would do the next best thing—protect Leah and Ben with his life if necessary.

Don't miss
UNDER THE LAWMAN'S PROTECTION
by Laura Scott,
available January 2015 wherever
Love Inspired® Suspense books and ebooks are sold.